dis*placed* PERSONS

Margie Taylor

Library and Archives Canada Cataloguing in Publication
Taylor, Margie
Displaced persons / Margie Taylor.

ISBN 1-896300-82-0 (pbk.)

I. Title.

PS8589.A90725D47 2004   C813'.54   C2004-903613-0

Board editor: Lynne Van Luven
Cover and interior design: Ruth Linka
Author photograph: Rosey Brenan
Cover photograph: Horst Ehricht

NeWest Press acknowledges the support of the Canada Council for the Arts and
the Alberta Foundation for the Arts, and the Edmonton Arts Council for our
publishing program. We also acknowledge the financial support of the
Government of Canada through the Book Publishing Industry
Development Program (BPIDP) for our publishing activities.

NeWest Press
201–8540–109 Street
Edmonton, Alberta T6G 1E6
(780) 432-9427
www.newestpress.com

1 2 3 4 5 07 06 05 04

PRINTED AND BOUND IN CANADA
ON ANCIENT-FOREST-FRIENDLY PAPER

dis*placed*
PERSONS
Margie Taylor

For her continuing support of women, and writers,
and especially women writers,
this book is dedicated to Margaret Phillips,
owner of The Northern Woman's Bookstore, Thunder Bay, Ontario

ALL BIOGRAPHY IS AUTOBIOGRAPHY. WE TELL OUR STORIES by focusing the lens on someone else. This particular story starts with a beautiful girl and a cello in front of the grain elevators, down by the docks; it ends with the blast of a 12-gauge shotgun in a small cabin by the lake.

The beginning and ending are no problem. It's the in-between bits I'm not sure about.

January 1969:

She told me she'd been freezing out there—freezing her ass off in a shocking pink shirt and matching ski pants, courtesy of Bev's Boutique, not that Bev had any idea she'd supplied it. She'd chosen this particular outfit because it played up her velvet blue eyes and she could wear the shirt out, to cover her butt; she now wished like hell she'd found something warmer than 100 per cent polyester. Twenty below and a wind whipping off the lake that would freeze the ass off—well, an ass. Her eyes watered. Little icicles formed on her eyelashes. She worried her mascara would run.

She wondered if the owner of Bev's Boutique would recognize this pantsuit when the magazine came out. Perhaps she'd call the police. Then again, it was unlikely; all pantsuits look the same, and it would be Bev's word against hers.

She hadn't thought about the weather when she got the call from Delia, the perpetually youthful, downright chirpy little thing who ran the modelling agency.

"Wear something bright," she'd said. "Something in pastel, if you can. Pink is good on you, or baby blue—with your hair and eyes, you'll look stunning."

Delia said it was a magazine shoot—"a national magazine

cover, dear—very exciting"—and the photographer had asked for a look that was virginal but sophisticated.

"Of course I immediately thought of you," Delia said. Not much money, unfortunately, these things were for prestige more than anything. But so good for the career—"It will look wonderful in your book, just a terrific opportunity."

Delia might have saved her breath—Tina did not need coaxing. She'd been waiting for this all her life. She didn't give a shit about the money—she'd have done it for free. Five years of stupid local fashion shows, squeezed into girdles and high heels, parading up and down makeshift catwalks set up in hockey arenas, smiling out at small-town matrons and their chubby, unattractive daughters. Served tea and tiny sandwiches afterwards, made boring small talk, smiled hard enough to give herself a headache. This was what it was all leading up to. Stand out on a pile of rocks in the middle of winter for a couple of hours? Hell, she'd pose stark naked with this cello up her ass if it got her the cover of a national magazine.

The photographer had called the night before, tracked her down at Michael's apartment and asked her to meet him down at the harbour at ten o'clock the next morning. He had a faint foreign accent; she thought he was German.

Quietly, so Michael wouldn't hear her, she told the photographer how much she was looking forward to working with him, how it would be nice to get to know him a little beforehand.

"I'd be happy to come up to your hotel room for a minute or two," she said. "We could have a drink together, talk about the shoot. Really, it's no trouble."

There was a pause while he considered the offer. She racked her brain for an excuse to give Michael—she could say she'd been called in to work.

"I'm tired," the photographer said. "We will talk tomorrow." Then he wished her goodnight and hung up.

Margie Taylor

The next morning at the grain dock, he was pleasant enough but all business.

"You are on time," he said, checking his watch. "Good, that is very good. We will have until twelve o'clock, providing the light is with us."

He wanted her sitting on a rock down by the water, holding the cello in front of her and gazing out at the horizon, supposedly for musical inspiration. There was an assistant with him, a skinny young guy with a moustache, whose job it was to pour coffee from a Thermos in the back of the car and wink at her in what she assumed was meant to be an encouraging manner. She sat there, smiling into the distance, trying to keep the cello from falling over on to its side— it was surprisingly heavy; the women who played these things must have great biceps—while the photographer fiddled with the camera.

Eventually he looked up and said, "Art and the working class."

She nodded, smiled sweetly, and adjusted her grip on the cello.

"You get?"

Again, she smiled. Shook her head. She didn't get.

He turned and waved an arm in the direction of the city.

"Contrast," he said. "A beautiful young woman plays the cello"—this with a nod in her direction—"and in the background we see the magnificent grain elevators, the largest in the world. Symbol of the working classes. The masses and the music. You get?"

Now she got. It was the theme of this cover—culture in a lunch-bucket town. Toronto would love it.

A cloud passed overhead and the photographer—Hans, his name was, or Heinz—said they'd take a break. The assistant placed his sheepskin coat over her shoulders, gave her a wink, and told her she was doing fine.

"You're a trooper," he said. "A real trooper."

Another wink and now she saw that it was a nervous tic, not a come-on.

"You are cold."

It was a statement, not a question; she shook her head.

"Oh, no, not at all. I'm fine. I'm just fine." Her teeth were chattering and her fingers were now too numb to feel the bow she was clutching. If she'd known about this shoot even a week earlier, she could have gone shoplifting during the January sales and found herself a pantsuit with a warmer lining. At the very least she should have taken Michael up on his offer of a pair of long johns. At the time, though, they hadn't sounded very elegant.

"Good." Heinz—or Hans—rubbed his hands together, glanced up at the sky. "We wait another twenty minutes or so, the clouds will pass. We get a better light."

She shifted slightly on her rocky perch. A pair of seagulls flew overhead, pierced the silence with their cries. She wrapped the jacket around her more tightly, and waited for the light.

※ ※ ※

1

OCTOBER 1997. PEBBLE BEACH, LAKE SUPERIOR

I GREW UP NEXT TO A LAKE, SURROUNDED BY BUSH
and rocks and water, in a town of mill workers, railway workers,
teachers, doctors, and businessmen. The Italians ruled the East
End, the Finns organized the unions and the co-ops. A covered
wooden shelter marked Intercity, where the buses turned
around and you waited in the cold for the Main Line bus to take
you from one part of town to the other. There was a synagogue
and a Greek Orthodox church and two churches on the Indian
reserve, just outside town. I grew up wanting to get away, and
so I married a Welsh university professor and moved halfway
across the country, settled on the west coast, had children and
raised them to adulthood.

This past June I placed the following ad in my hometown
newspaper:

> WANTED TO RENT: Furnished cabin, not too
> rustic, with view of the lake, from September to
> Christmas. Suitable for woman writer with
> friendly, well-behaved dog.

An excitable woman named Marjorie Henderson called me
in Vancouver.

"Our place is fully furnished," she said, thrilled at the possibility of renting the place to a real live writer. "We've been
staying out there year-round, but Harry can't take the cold—
well, he had a tough time last year, a double bypass. He's fine
now, but you never know, life is short, right? So we're heading
down to Phoenix at the end of August. You could rent it all winter or just part, whatever suits. The view of the lake is wonderful; I'm sure you'll find it very inspiring."

When I reminded her I wanted to bring my dog, Marjorie assured me the dog would love the place too.

"We have a dog ourselves," she said. "A darling little Jack Russell. She's Harry's dog, really, they just adore each other. And Harry's taught her the sweetest tricks. He just blows a whistle, and Coquette—that's the dog—she sits up and begs and rolls over and plays dead. It's too bad we're going to be gone when you get here—the dogs could play together."

And so, in September, after David has left for England, I pack up my clothes and my laptop computer, settle Jake, the dog, in the back of the car, and drive across the country. It feels like an adventure, although the only drama consists of swerving to avoid oncoming drivers as they head towards me on the wrong side of the highway. I pass hitchhikers and feel bad about not picking them up—I would have, a few years ago, and still would if the weather were rotten. But the sun shines overhead from the coast to Thunder Bay, so I drive past my would-be companions and silently beg their pardon.

The trip takes four days. The dog sleeps most of the way, waking up when he has to pee, or when I stop to get gas. I fiddle with the radio dial, trying to find good talk or interesting music, but eventually give up. The country's too big, the radio waves can't keep up with the distances involved. You can't even find the old country and western stations anymore; in a misguided attempt to please the aging boomers, they've switched to soft rock and easy listening. As our bodies grow flabby and our eyesight gets worse, it seems our musical tastes deteriorate as well.

I fill the void by talking to the dog.

"You're probably wondering why we're doing this, Jake," I say, passing an advertisement for the town of Biggar, Saskatchewan. ("New York's big, but we're Biggar!")

"You got in the car two days ago thinking we were going for a walk, and here we are, still driving. So what are we doing, you wonder? Well, that's a good question."

According to my son, Adam, I'm running away. He called from California the night before I left and said if I wanted to do research, couldn't I just get on the Internet? Did I really have to drive all the way to Thunder Bay and live in a cottage all winter?

"They're called camps," I told him. "Cottage is putting on airs. If you say cottage, people know you're from Toronto."

"Be careful, Mom," Adam said. "It's a big lake, and you're not a good swimmer."

David taught the children to swim when they were little. I sat on the bleachers and watched, marvelling at his patience. He was a gentle, untiring teacher, and under his tutelage they excelled in the water. He would have taught me to swim, too, had I been willing to learn.

"That's the thing about David," I say, continuing my one-sided conversation with the dog. "He loves to teach. And he's good at it. I should know—I was his star pupil."

David has had many star pupils since then. Young women, mostly, slouched in their seats in jeans and short, cropped T-shirts. Their tummies are flat, their breasts are firm and they never, ever think about whether the light is flattering. Of course he loves being a teacher.

By the time I reach the Manitoba border, I'm driving in silence. I don't want to talk to the dog about David, I don't want to think about why I left home.

※ ※ ※

The sun is setting in my rear-view mirror as I arrive on the outskirts of Thunder Bay. Ahead of me, a long stretch of fast-food restaurants, coffee shops, and motels welcome me home. None of this was here thirty years ago. There were still farms along this part of the highway, and the few houses set back from the road were considered "out in the country." I pass a couple of subdivisions where each home has at least two cars parked in front; there are no trees, but the houses are large and new.

The city's been franchised, since I lived here—the same stores, gas stations, burger chains and coffee shops you find in every town across the country. The shopping malls contain most of the same stores I know from Vancouver. If I stop to eat at any of the restaurants by the side of the highway, the food will taste exactly like it does in its west coast counterpart.

Ignoring the bypass, I take the slower route through town. The houses here are older, the stores are small and dark. A local department store has been torn down and replaced with a car park; the former post office is where you apply for unemployment insurance, and the best hotel in town has become a home for seniors. Compared to the shopping malls I passed on the highway, the downtown is deserted.

But the library is still standing, and the Anglican church— its bell tolls the quarter hour as I drive past the small, brown-brick house where my grandmother used to live. Her favourite bakery is closed, as is the bank where she worked before she was married. A lovely old home on the corner has been turned into a tea room and antique shop; Grandma would have liked a place like that.

As I leave the city behind, heading east on Lake Shore Drive, my spirits lift. The beauty of the landscape hasn't changed. This is not the place of my childhood, but the green and gold leaves of the birch trees still spread their triangular fingers against the sky, and the autumn moon rises to reflect itself in the black waters of the lake, just as it did thirty years ago.

2

OUT OF A COPSE OF WHITE BIRCH TREES, JAKE BOUNDS towards me. His tongue is hanging out of the side of his mouth like a discarded dishcloth. He gallops happily in my direction, managing at the final second to veer to the right and avoid a collision.

This is the high point of his day; from the moment he senses that I am awake, he's on high alert. I get up to use the bathroom and then climb back into bed; he fixes himself on the carpet beside me, poised for action, not sure if I am actually going to be so cruel as to go back to sleep or if I simply want to warm my toes before getting up for good.

If I close my eyes, pretend to ignore him, he settles on the floor with a sigh, shifting position every few minutes to let me know just how much it puts him out to have to wait on me like this, when any reasonable creature might realize he should be out sniffing, exploring, and excreting. Time and again he gets up, scratches an ear or makes a complete circle on the rug and settles down again, sighing. If I lie there long enough, he will abandon the passivity of this posture and begin to probe me with his nose, gently whining in a plea to stir myself. It would take a harder heart than mine to resist this performance, so I get up, pull on a sweatshirt and a pair of khakis, and open the front door.

He is out the door immediately, taking the three wooden steps in a single bounce, and racing through the long grass down to the lake. He won't go far; he's a Black Lab, after all, almost fourteen years old, and he likes to keep me in his sights. He knows, however, that I still have to get into my hiking boots

and lace them up (I sleep with my socks on out here, otherwise
my feet are blocks of ice in the morning), so he has a couple of
minutes to check out the shoreline and take a few cautious laps
from the lake. He won't go in—in that way he's not a true Lab,
his mixed breeding shows. The water is cold all year long and
now, in the middle of October, it is already beginning to hint at
the ice that will form on its surface in another month or so. The
only water this dog has ever enjoyed is the heated swimming
pool belonging to a friend of ours back in the city. When the
kids were younger and he was a pup, he used to leap into the
middle of the floating toys and mattresses and paddle around
for hours, to the delight of the children and the barely con-
cealed horror of their mothers.

In a few minutes, I'm ready. He ambles up from the water's
edge, and we're off on our morning ritual, striding along the
narrow dirt road that connects this cottage to the main road
where another dozen cabins are strung out along the shoreline.
The place where we're staying is nestled in a tiny cove with its
own rocky beach. At the front it faces the lake; at the back a
small yard, complete with patio and bird bath, has been carved
out of the bush. There are no immediate neighbours, and
although it takes less than twenty minutes to walk to the main
road, it feels remote and protected.

I can hear the dog making his way through the long, morn-
ing-damp grass, with frequent pauses to lift his leg against a
tree or sniff out a rabbit hole in the bank by the side of the road.
He runs to keep ahead of me, then gets sidetracked and falls
behind, but never too far. We have been out here for a month
now, he and I, and we both know by heart the route we will take.
We could vary it, I suppose, but I like the regularity of the pace
along this road, where the traffic is almost nonexistent, and the
dog can wander at will.

Margie Taylor

This is Indian summer, days of hazy skies and light winds, cool nights with a touch of frost. When I was growing up, I felt I only really came alive in the fall. The brilliance of the dying leaves, combined with the clear, pungent smell of organic matter, triggered an excitement within me. Each September I teetered on the brink of possibility, convinced that something new and quite wonderful was about to happen. The wind was different in the fall, it was more than just the natural movement of the air; it was an emissary from another, more exotic part of the world, and it spoke the language of sailors and gypsies, nomads of every kind. While others mourned the passing of summer, I felt I had been granted temporary membership into a fraternity of free spirits, pagan throwbacks to a time when the god of the harvest was propitiated with offerings of fruit and small animals.

The wind kindled a stirring-up within me, not unlike the sudden hormonal passions that got hold of me at unexpected moments, shaking me profoundly, then suddenly taking flight, leaving me agitated and unsettled.

Once we reach the main road, our view of the lake is interrupted at regular intervals by the cabins that straddle the beach. There is little uniformity among them, although I know from past experience they all contain certain elements: a deck, a sauna, a gas or propane barbecue, and a large window with a view of the lake. When I was young, these camps were inhabited only in the summer. There was no insulation in the walls and roofs, no protection from the deep, heart-stopping chill of northern winters. Only the occasional eccentric looking to get away from civilization lived out here all year long. It was half an hour into town, on a road that could be treacherous when the snow came.

Now the houses have been fixed up with central heating,

double glazing, indoor toilets, and electricity. The wood stove is still a fixture, however, and firewood is a big issue; it's as important as food. A load of white pine arrived at my back door last week, delivered by a man named Boo Montgomery. The wood is to be used in the handsome cast-iron stove at one end of the living room. On its own, this stove can heat the entire house, boil water for tea, allow a stew to simmer all afternoon. At night, I open a small vent in the front, and the fire, banked low, creates just enough heat to keep things cozy, providing a shaft of light in the darkness.

The first few nights I was uneasy because of that stove, woke up at three in the morning wondering if the chimney would catch fire, if I'd be burned to a crisp in my sleep. Now, though, I've learned to trust it. It has become a companion, like the dog, who begins each night lying in front of the stove and then moves progressively further away, until at last he scrambles on to my bed where it is just warm enough to be comfortable. When I wake in the middle of the night, the friendly glow from the front of the stove is reassuring: we are fine, we are not in danger, no harm will come to us tonight.

✕ ✕ ✕

The goal of our walk lies along a stretch of shoreline that used to be called Grandview Beach, about twenty minutes further east from Pebble Beach, where I'm staying. A pickup truck passes, and the dog and I move to the side of the road and wait. The driver waves; that much hasn't changed. *He probably thinks he knows me,* I think, but that may not be the case. He may simply be friendly, in the way country people are immediately friendly on one level and permanently hostile on another. Or he may just be waving because I'm a woman with a dog.

Tina's place—what used to be her place—is halfway down Grandview Beach Avenue. To get there, we pass a twelve-foot iron fence, topped with barbed wire, which guards a very small house and a large, extremely aggressive dog. The dog, which appears to be a cross between a Rottweiler and a Russian wolfhound, sets up the most incredible din the moment he sees us, but always stops barking the minute we get past his property. My own dog keeps his distance, the mammoth fence notwithstanding; his policy is one of avoidance, and the older he gets the more firmly he sticks to that rule.

Number 6 is another hundred yards down the road, a tiny, one-storey dwelling with a flat roof, and small, unrevealing windows. I always thought it was a pity the windows weren't larger, considering the spectacular view they might have offered. A generous sundeck wraps around the front and one side, built by one of Tina's ex-boyfriends. Rob, I think his name was. Tall, blond, good-looking, and a very good carpenter. He fixed up the sauna, too, rebuilt it and then brought his girlfriends down in the evenings and entertained them in that hot, steamy space. Tina didn't mind; she was never jealous of men once she'd stopped having sex with them.

The deck has been recently painted a dark, forest green to match the colour of the old front door. Someone has built a couple of window boxes and nailed them under the two small windows that look out on to the lake. The lawn needs cutting, and weeds are beginning to push their way up through the cracks in the front steps. Whoever lives here now doesn't do a lot of yardwork.

The sauna is still standing, but doesn't look as if it has been used for years as anything except a ramshackle tool shed. I pried the door open the first day I was here, just to see, and it was dark and filthy inside, with a few rakes and an old-fashioned

lawn mower parked in one corner. The stove was gone, and the
bench where we used to sweat was piled with half-empty bags of
potting soil and an assortment of plant pots, spades, trowels,
and watering cans. Dust and cobwebs shrouded everything.
Flies crawled in through the cracks in the wood, seeking a warm
place to escape from the encroaching chill; I closed the door and
left them in peace.

The dog and I make our way down the overgrown path to
the shore where, as always, he tests the water briefly then sets
out to explore the shrubbery at the water's edge. I sit down on
a large flat rock and stare out across the water. It's a view I could
paint from memory, even after all these years away.

Directly ahead of me, about ten miles out, a rocky finger of
land dominates the horizon: Nanabijou, Spirit of the Deep Sea
Water, who lost his life in a powerful storm and was turned into
stone by the gods. The storm wasn't even his fault. He had given
his people a gift: high on Thunder Cape was the entrance to a
rich silver mine, and as long as the Ojibway kept the secret to
themselves, the precious metal was theirs for the taking. But a
young Sioux scout discovered the secret of the location and gave
it away to a couple of unscrupulous trappers. When the white
men brought their digging tools to the area, the skies turned
dark and the wind and rain beat down for three days. When the
storm finally receded, the silver mine was buried in a hundred
feet of water and Nanabijou was dead. He lies on his back, arms
folded, stretched out into the bay, a constant reminder of the
power of Nature, and her daughter, the great inland sea.

The first book—no, let's be honest—the *only* book I ever
read about water was *Peter Freuchen's Book of the Seven Seas*. It
was a Christmas present from my mother to my father, the year
I was eight. Dad thumbed through it carefully, showing me the
black and white drawings of ancient ships and sea serpents, let-

ting me take the book to the kitchen table, where I was mindful not to smudge the pages as I turned them. From this book I learned that the deep sea waters, which appear silent and practically barren, are teeming with life, some of it dating back millions of years.

Freuchen tells the story of the Cape Town fisherman who, in 1938, caught a bright blue fish, five feet in length, with a big head. The fish, which scientists named "Latimeria," was supposed to have become extinct millions of years before humans appeared in the world. Since then dozens of these bluefish have turned up, and one was kept alive in a tank for more than three months. "Where," Freuchen wonders, "had they been for nearly 20 million years?" Where, indeed?

The lake always frightened me. If a long-extinct coelacanth could turn up off the coast of South Africa, who's to say something similarly terrible might not appear out of the icy waters of Thunder Bay?

I went out on boats in the city harbour but not far, just to the edge of the breakwater, where the deep water began. Far enough, as far as I was concerned. This is not a mild-mannered, fishing-hole kind of lake. This is an inland sea, a freshwater ocean deeper than any other on earth, so cold in places that it does not give up its dead, but keeps them locked forever in a frigid, liquid crypt. Its average water temperature is four degrees Celsius; its maximum depth is 1,333 feet; it contains 3 quadrillion gallons of water. Who could feel completely safe with such potency, such depth?

I shiver as the wind picks up, although I don't think it's gone colder. If I was superstitious, I'd say it was Tina's shadow passing over me, reminding me of the last night I stayed here. We sat on the sofa, drinking Southern Comfort and listening to Janis Joplin. Tina had seen Janis at a concert in Winnipeg the summer of 1970, one of the last performances she gave before she died. Her theory was that if Janis had been prettier, she'd still be alive.

Janis died from alcohol and heroin; I said I didn't see what being pretty had to do with it.

"She went to college, and they voted her 'Ugliest Man on Campus.' Don't you think that hurt? She drank and took drugs to cover up the pain. You could tell she was in pain, just watching her."

"So if she'd been prettier, she'd have stayed in Port Arthur, Texas, and married a used-car salesman. And we wouldn't be sitting here listening to her right now."

"Lousy for us," she said. "But better for her, don't you think?"

"You're making an assumption that what she really wanted was a husband."

Tina shook her head. "Not a husband—a lover. Someone to hold her and keep her from thinking about bad things."

"I like to think she was braver than that."

"She was. She was possibly the bravest woman in the music business. But she was still a woman."

She reached out and turned up the volume.

"Listen to the words, Alex: 'Didn't I make you feel like you were the only man? Didn't I give you nearly everything that a woman possibly can?'"

I jumped up and threw open my arms, in mock appeal to an imaginary audience: "Honey, you *know* I did!"

Tina joined me—onstage, so to speak—and we sang together, belting out the lines with a theatrical flourish that would have made Janis proud. Or fall down laughing.

And each time I tell myself that I think I've had enough,
But I'm gonna show you, baby, that a woman can be tough!
I want you to come on, come on, come on, come on, and take it,

Take another little piece of my heart now, baby!
You know you got it if it makes you feel good.

That's the memory: when I picked up the phone and Liz told me Tina was dead, that's what I remembered. Dancing around the living room of that little cabin, her arm around my waist, waving our empty glasses in the air. Singing a Janis song.

The dog has had enough. He comes over and pushes his muzzle into my hand.

"All right, boy, let's go."

With an effort, I get to my feet and head up the grassy slope to the road behind the house. Five weeks ago I stopped at a music store on my way out of Vancouver and bought the *Cheap Thrills* CD, thinking it would be fun to play it on the long drive east. It's still in its plastic wrapping; I'm not ready to hear "Piece of My Heart" just yet.

3

Back at the house the green light on the telephone blinks. It's an event for me to have a message, unless it's from one of the kids. Kate's at university in Montreal and Adam's going to school in San Diego. Neither phones during the daytime.

I feel a pang when I think of my children, so far away, involved in their own lives. You tell yourself it's what you've always wanted for them, independence, the ability to survive on their own. You don't know that when the time comes you'll feel like a part of you is cut off and buried somewhere, but still experiencing sensation. It's the Catch-22 of motherhood: if you're a good parent and do your job well, your children will leave you the very first chance they get.

I should have been Jewish; I want to weep and wail and guilt them into coming home, where I can watch over them and keep them safe. And then I remind myself that I, too, have left home; if they should decide to give up their dreams and scurry back to mother, she is no longer there. As Adam says, I've run away.

The phone message is from a woman named Joan whom I met Saturday night at a party in town. She wants to know my "schedule" this week, when we can have lunch together. Her voice, which is cheerful in a manner that sounds rehearsed, makes me feel guilty—this is a woman who makes plans and books appointments. She leaves me her phone number, twice, and signs off with "Toodle-oo, talk to you soon."

I place the receiver in its cradle and wish I hadn't given her my number. I don't want to "do lunch," I don't want to make

Margie Taylor

new friends. And I wish to hell Liz hadn't thrown me that party.

Nobody ever believes me when I tell them I hate parties. They assume, because I'm a columnist, because I've been on TV, that I live for the limelight. Liz, of all people, should know better.

I had decided to finish my drink and leave as discreetly as possible, when I was accosted by a large attractive woman with red hair pulled back from her broad, freckled face.

"Hang on—don't I know you?"

The redhead was dressed in a glitzy jacket of black satin and gold brocade and a pair of tight-fitting black capris. Her fingernails shrieked with glossy red paint and she wore three or four rings on each hand, one of which was pointing in my direction.

"You're Alex Cooper. I knew you looked familiar."

Before I could respond, she reached for my hand and held it in a firm but not unpleasant grip.

"Joan Dawson," she said. "Liz told me you'd be here. I'm so glad to finally meet you."

Instead of releasing me, she pulled me down the hall to Liz's bedroom and shut the door.

"We can talk in here. Where it's quiet."

Something must have shown in my face, because she smiled and said in a stage whisper, "It's okay, I'm not going to bite you."

"Oh, no, I didn't mean—"

I always get flustered if I feel I've been rude. I've spent most of my adult life turning myself inside out in an effort to prove how much I like people. Only now and then it comes out that, for the most part, I don't.

Besides the bed, the room contained a small couch, more of a loveseat, really, upholstered in pale cream hopsacking just a shade darker than the painted walls and woodwork. Liz has turned her tiny home in the north end of town into something out of *House and Garden.* I miss the old comfort of the place, when you could flop into a chair and put your feet up. Now that her sons are grown and moved out on their own, Liz just has too much time on her hands. All that manic energy's been sublimated into home décor.

The redhead settled herself on the loveseat and patted the space beside her.

"Sit down. Just for a minute. I'm dying to talk to you."

Shifting in beside her, I was aware of an almost overpowering scent—somewhere between vanilla and roses. Everything about this woman was larger than life. Tiny, insubstantial people make me nervous. They're like small dogs that snap at your heels and threaten to bite you if you're not careful. Give me big and solid any day. Big men, especially, who can sweep you up and swing you around. And protect you.

She took my hand again and gave it a comforting squeeze. "I never miss your column in the Globe," she confided. "I'm a huge fan. *Huge.* I mean, you have no idea. But I guess you hear that all the time."

I shook my head. "No, not really. Thank you."

She sipped her drink and studied me for a moment, before telling me that in her opinion, my column was the best thing in the whole paper. "What do they pay you? It better be a fortune, because you're worth it."

I told her the column's been dropped—new management, a different look, going for a younger readership.

"But it's fine," I said, launching into the speech I've been giving since the axe fell in June: a door closes, a window opens up. Fifteen years in one place is long enough for anyone, I needed a change even if I didn't know it. Now I can finally sit

Margie Taylor

down and write that book I've been carrying around in my head for the past decade. I've said this so often I'm almost beginning to believe it.

Joan heard me out, then told me she knows about the book. Liz told her I've come back to write about Tina, who died out at the lake, twenty years ago.

"I knew her that summer," Joan said. "Did Liz tell you? I knew her boyfriend, too, Conrad Schaeffer. We grew up in the same part of town. Which is not something I brag about, believe me."

And so I asked her the question.

"What do you think happened to her?"

"It's hard to say—Conrad had some pretty unpleasant friends. What do *you* think?"

"I think the woman I knew would not have taken a gun, put it to her forehead and pulled the trigger. I can't believe she would have been willing to destroy her face, no matter how desperate she felt."

Joan nodded. "Yeah, that's pretty much what I've always thought."

We sipped our wine in silence—it's a depressing subject. Joan drained her glass and set it down on the tiny glass table beside her.

"Can I ask you something?" Joan leaned forward to look directly into my eyes. "We just met, I don't know you and you don't know me, but I have a feeling we can be honest with each other. Why do you want to write about her? Do you think you're going to be able to figure out what happened? Nobody'll ever prove anything, you know."

"It's not that. I'm not trying to write an exposé."

"Then what? I mean, this was a woman we both knew, a long time ago. I haven't thought about her in years. And as much as I liked her, we both know she was no heroine. She was hooked on speed, she ripped people off, and she slept with all the wrong men. Tina was a bit of a wacko, if you want to know the truth. So why write about her?"

For a moment, I hesitated. It was a direct question, it deserved a direct answer. The thing is, you don't always know how truthful you can be in these situations. It's hard enough being honest with yourself, let alone levelling with someone you hardly know.

"She intrigued me, I guess. She didn't behave like any of the people I knew. She wasn't a feminist, she didn't seem to want a career, but she wasn't into marriage and babies, either. She was just out there on her own path, and of course, she behaved very badly. Which is what I think I liked about her— her behaving badly. It was like belonging to a club of some kind. I don't regret dropping out of the club, but sometimes I wonder what would have happened if I'd stayed."

This answer, as incomplete as it may be, seems to satisfy her.

"We should talk," she says. "You've got me thinking about Tina again, about the summer she died. We should definitely go for lunch. I'll call you."

And she did.

✕ ✕ ✕

The Starlite Motor Inn, where Joan has suggested we meet, used to be a high-class restaurant. My sister worked there years ago and she gave me two rules to follow when dining out in this town: first, never send anything back to the kitchen. Cooks take out their wrath on dissatisfied customers in despicable ways.

"Tell them you don't want it, and order something else,"

she said, "or leave it on your plate. But don't send it back."

Rule number two: don't order the lobster. The main feature of the dining room at the Starlite was a large tank containing three lobsters. You were supposed to walk up to it and pick out the one you wanted; the waiter would fish out your lobster and take it back to the kitchen, where the chef would proceed to cook you up a frozen one. After you left, your lobster would be put back in its tank. My sister said those three lobsters had been there practically forever—they were so old, she said, their shells were like rock. If they ever did get cooked, she was certain they'd be inedible.

The Starlite has changed hands several times over the years. It's still a motel, but now it's owned by a chain, and the lobsters are long since gone. It would be nice to think that somebody had returned them to the ocean, but as we're three thousand miles from either coast, it seems unlikely.

This is not a place I would have chosen to meet, with its view of the parking lot and the highway just beyond it. But this is Joan's treat. Later, I know, we'll argue over the bill, the way women do, and she'll win. She's used to getting her own way, you can tell.

"Try the soup," she says. "They make it themselves."

"It says that on the menu but I never believe it."

"Well, in this case it's true," she counters. "It's the reason I come here."

She's right. When the soup comes—wild mushroom—it is heavenly, fragrant and creamy and served with crusty rolls and a generous serving of whipped butter, rather than those despicable little pats. The house wine, too, is a pleasant surprise, with a lusty, smoky flavour. Five minutes into the meal I find I'm enjoying myself and wondering why I'm so reluctant to meet new people.

Between bites of her roll and sips of wine, Joan tells me she remembers me from years ago, when we were both at university.

"You were younger than me, of course. And you had the best-looking boyfriend. Michael Somebody."

"Donovan."

"Michael Donovan. Right. He was gorgeous."

She wants to know if I married him. I say no, far too quickly, as if the idea is absurd, out of the question. But Michael did ask me to marry him once, in a casual, offhand way, the way he'd approach anything that really mattered to him. I laughed at the time because I wasn't sure he meant it, but later I regretted it. Not that I wanted to marry him. I didn't want to marry anybody. But I shouldn't have laughed. Michael could hold a grudge for a very long time.

"He was Tina's boyfriend," I tell her, "before we met. That's how I got to know him, through Tina. She introduced us."

"So who *did* you marry?"

It's a natural enough question but I resent it a little, as if it is only too obvious that I must have married somebody.

"Nobody you'd know." And then, because that sounds a little curt, I tell her his name is David and he's Welsh. As if that somehow explains things.

"Are you divorced?"

"Oh, no. I mean, not really. He's in England for a year, on a fellowship."

"I see," she says, and maybe she does. People often understand more than you give them credit for.

"Tell me," I ask, "how did you meet Tina?"

"I was working in a little store called The Kama Sutra. Actually, I was part owner of the place. Do you remember it?"

I remember it: a tiny hole-in-the-wall on the north side of

town; its window featured a mannequin dressed in exotic lin-
gerie. I never had the nerve to go in.

"We were way ahead of our time—sit down, have a cup of
tea, browse through our catalogue of sex toys. My partner and I
ran it for almost three years. Just long enough to go broke."

According to Joan, Tina came into the store one day looking for a negligee, something sexy that would conceal the fact
that she'd put on weight—again.

"I don't know why," Joan says, "but we hit it off right away.
We just clicked, you know? And then when I realized this
boyfriend she was talking about was Conrad Schaeffer, whom I
practically grew up with—well, we just seemed to be meant to
be friends."

She makes large, graceful gestures with her hands while
talking, like a Frenchman, my father would have said. Her
hands are unusually slender for a big woman, the nails too long
and perfectly shaped to be real. My own fingers are short and
stubby, like my father's. Writers' hands. I tend to keep them out
of sight, ashamed of my fingernails, which I'm embarrassed to
say I still chew occasionally. She must know her hands are
attractive; she's decorated them with a half-dozen rings, one of
which—the one on her baby finger—stands out. A large, oval-
cut diamond, held in place by an ornately carved silver band in
the shape of two snakes, one on each side. Difficult to ignore
even if the lights from the restaurant were not glinting from its
surface, hitting you right in the eye.

Tina was living out at the lake that summer, and Joan drove
out to visit her. What she remembers about the place was that
every cupboard, every drawer was crammed full of pills.
Uppers, downers, speed—you name it.

"It shocked me," she says. "And I didn't think I was all that
shockable. She'd told me she took diet pills—she said she got

hooked on them when she was a teenager. And of course everyone smoked pot. But this—this was something else."

In fact, Tina and Conrad made their money selling prescription drugs. Tina had a deal with a pharmacist downtown, who kept her supplied with pills.

"She implied it was a sex-for-drugs kind of thing," Joan says. "The drugstore owner caught her shoplifting and was going to call the cops. She'd been caught before and was afraid she'd end up in jail this time, so they worked out an arrangement."

The waitress brings our coffee to the table and asks if we want dessert.

"Order the chocolate cake," Joan says. "I'd love to watch you eat it." She must hear how odd that sounds because she adds, "I've been on a diet for seventeen years. I get vicarious pleasure watching other people eat."

But I'm not much of a dessert eater myself, so Joan asks for the bill. As we sip our coffee, she talks about the last time she saw Tina.

"It was a Sunday, the first weekend in August. She called me around noon, asked me to come out to the camp and have dinner. I didn't really want to, to be honest. I was tired and it was a long drive. But she sounded sad and I knew she was spending a lot of time out there on her own. I don't know what Conrad was doing, but he was never around. So in the end I gave in."

When Joan got there the place was a mess; the stereo was playing at full volume. The dog hadn't been fed—he was nosing around the kitchen, looking for food. The first thing Joan did was turn down the music. Then she refilled the dog's water bowl and opened a tin of dog food.

Tina was lying on the couch, watching television with the sound turned off. She told Joan to help herself to a beer from the fridge, which she did, then she went and sat down next to Tina on the couch. After a while Tina got up and went into the kitchen, coming back a few minutes later with a double handful of small bottles, each of which contained an assortment of dif-ferent-coloured pills. She set them down on the coffee table and lined them up in a row.

"My drugs of choice," she told Joan, and laughed. "You'd think it was candy, wouldn't you, if you didn't know."

"She held up each bottle," Joan says, "and told me what was in it and what it did to you. It was like listening to some weird kind of pharmacist. She knew all about them. Anything she didn't know, she had this big book, kind of a druggie's encyclo-pedia, sitting on the coffee table."

After explaining the contents of each one of the bottles, Tina pried off the lids and took a single pill out of each, making a lit-tle pile of them there on the table. And then she swallowed them. Every single one of them.

"There must have been eight or ten pills in all. I thought she'd freak out right there on the spot—or drop dead. But she didn't. She just curled up on the couch with her head on my shoulder and went to sleep."

And that was it. Joan sat there for a while, sipping her beer, and watching the TV with the sound off. Eventually she decided that if she didn't get something to eat she was going to pass out. So she placed a blanket over Tina and left.

The waitress comes by with our bill. Before I can reach for it, Joan has scooped it up and handed the girl her MasterCard. When the waitress is gone, she continues:

"It was about a week after that that Conrad died. A couple of weeks later, she was gone too. Both of them dead, just like that. It was sad. But it wasn't really surprising. I think I'd been expecting to read something like that almost as long as I'd known her."

✂ ✂ ✂

In the doorway of the restaurant, we stop to button our coats. It was mild when we arrived just before noon; now the sun has disappeared, and the sky looms grey and ominous, looks like it might snow. The thought revives the old dread within me, the fear of being trapped in the cabin by the lake, the roads impassable, and me cut off and alone.

"I hate to think of her out there," Joan says, as if she knows what I'm thinking. "All by herself, Conrad dead, all those crazy things going through her head. It must have been awful."

"She told me once she never expected to live beyond forty," I say. "I think it was because of her mother—did she ever tell you the story?"

The way Tina told it, her mother had been beautiful when she was younger—"notoriously beautiful" was the way Tina put it—and extremely vain. She was married, briefly, to Tina's father, but he died. She married again, had Tina's stepsister, Marianne, and again found herself a widow. Finally, she met and married a Canadian soldier based in Germany and ended up moving to northwestern Ontario, a long way from Germany and the Black Forest.

At any rate, so the story went, the day her mother turned forty she discovered her very first wrinkle. At which point she went into her bedroom and stayed there. Never came out again, just sat in the dark mourning the loss of her looks. Joan listens while I relate this, watching me with an odd expression.

"I've always thought it explained a lot about Tina, don't you think? Her mother giving up on life like that, all because of a wrinkle."

"It would, I guess, if it were true. I met her mother at Safeway that summer—Tina introduced me. A very sweet, ordinary-looking woman. She was visiting from Toronto and the two of them had gone to bingo the night before and her mother won fifty dollars. And her mom said she went all the time in Toronto but her luck was always better here. She was an absolutely normal person, Alex. Nothing the least bit strange about her."

Joan pulls on a pair of leather driving gloves and glances up at the sky.

"She was full of shit, that girl," she says, "but I liked her."

"I know," I tell her. "So did I."

4

As always, the dream begins when I am already knee-deep in the lake, the cold water coursing around me. A full moon, everything is illuminated. Someone is just a little ahead of me, laughing, urging me on. As I walk further out, I feel the mud squishing between my toes, lovely and cool, like Plasticine. The water gets deeper, it rushes past me, amid rocks and dangerous passages. It becomes a river, and I see a small island perhaps ten yards away. I know if I can just make it to there I'll be safe, but although I push towards it, I get no closer. And the water is rising.

There is something soothing about the feel of the water rushing between my legs, and also something powerful. The water begins to climb steadily; I turn to look back at the shore and the telephone rings.

"You sound sleepy. I didn't wake you, did I? I thought you'd be up."

It's David, calling from Cardiff.

"I was. I am. I just fell back asleep for a moment. How are you?"

"Freezing," he says. "I came up to Mum's on Friday, and it's been raining all weekend. And she refuses to turn up the central heating."

"Put on a sweater," I tell him, and he laughs. David's mother has a very Welsh sense of economy. An extra sweater—jumper, she calls it—is her cure for everything.

He starts telling me about a paper he presented at the West Midlands psychology conference: Organizational Psychology and the Potential for Human Achievement. It's from the book he's working on. I try to pay attention. As always, when he's far away I find it an effort to think about him, to believe he still exists. He once told me I was just like the dog, who forgets all about you when you're not around, writhes in ecstasy when you return, and within minutes has forgotten you were ever away.

"How can you know that? You don't know he forgets about us, you can't read his mind."

He said a dog's brain was the size of an orange and Jake wasn't capable of missing anybody. My husband is brilliant in the classroom but he knows nothing about animals.

This difference of opinion about dogs is just one of the ways in which David and I are different. It never mattered, in the early years. He used to take a perverse pride in my lack of interest in all things scientific; he thought of me as "a free spirit."

"Look at her," he told friends over dinner one night. "She's bright and educated and over thirty and she still believes the Big Bang is only a theory."

He said it proudly, as if announcing I'd won the Nobel Prize. He married me thinking I was so different from Jane, his first wife, only to discover how similar we were, under the skin. He must sometimes feel cheated. But isn't that how it is with marriage? If you stay together long enough, at some point each of you will feel you got less than you bargained for.

"How about you?" he wants to know. "How's the writing going? What are you finding out?"

There was a time when I shared everything with David; he was my editor, my arbiter. If David liked my work, that was all that mattered. Now I hoard my writing, give out little bits and pieces grudgingly, like a miser.

"Not much. I've met a woman I think is going to be helpful.

Her name's Joan Dawson and she used to run a sex shop here in town."

"Sounds very risqué."

"She's not, actually."

"Well, I hope you're not giving away any trade secrets."

"She remembers me from university. When I lived with Michael."

"Ah, the incomparable Mr. Donovan. Funny how his name keeps coming up."

"Everybody's name comes up eventually, David. Michael's no more important than anyone else."

We don't have much more to say to each other after that. He asks me what I've heard from the kids, I ask about his mother, there's a pause, he tells me a funny story about his train trip from Paddington station. Just before we say goodbye, he says he misses me.

"I miss you, too."

It's an automatic response, the kind you make when conversation is less about communicating than about reassurance. If missing someone means you feel incomplete with them gone, then the truth is that I miss my children; I do not particularly miss my husband.

He's right about one thing, though: Michael Donovan's name does keep coming up.

✂ ✂ ✂

I knew about Michael before I actually met him. He'd gone out with Tina around the time she did the modelling stint for the magazine; she told me they'd bought property together out on the lake. By the time I got to know her, Michael had left Thunder Bay—because of Tina. At least, that was the impression I got. She implied he'd been heartbroken when she broke up with him, and had headed down to Mexico. He was living in Puerto Vallarta, hanging out on the beach and learning Spanish.

I ran into her after class one day and she said she'd heard from Michael—he'd run out of money and was coming back to Thunder Bay. She said she'd introduce us.

"You'll like him," she told me. "Everybody likes Michael. He's very sweet."

"If he's so wonderful, why'd you break up with him?"

"I wasn't in love with him," she said. "I loved him, but I wasn't *in* love with him. He couldn't stand that he cared for me more than I cared for him. He can't forgive me for that. But we're good friends."

I caught a glimpse of him a week later, from the window of a car. He was standing at the bus stop with a friend, smoking a cigarette and laughing about something, and I knew it was him. I remember that as the car I was in passed him, he smiled at me and that smile was a kind of a blow to the heart.

When he walked into the university cafeteria the following day, I literally started to tremble. He had high cheekbones and soft brown hair that parted in the middle and came down to his shoulders. He had a tan—unheard of in Thunder Bay in the winter—and his eyes were almond-shaped, like an Egyptian painting. If a man can be called beautiful, Michael was it.

He was with Tina and she brought him over to the table where I was sitting.

"This is Alex," she told him. "You should ask her out."

And he did.

He took me to a movie sponsored by the campus film society. It was very dark and artsy. Halfway through we agreed we both hated it and left. Out in the hallway, he asked if I'd like to come out to his camp on Grandview Beach. It was snowing and the roads were bad, but I said yes.

By the time we turned off the road into his driveway, my teeth were chattering, and it was only partly because the heater in his car wasn't working. I hardly knew him; had I been foolish to come all this way with him? And the cabin, when it emerged out of the darkness, seemed small and second-rate. When he referred to "my place on the lake," it had sounded more grand.

Once inside, Michael busied himself building up the fire and retrieving a bottle of wine from the cooler. I stood by the window with my coat on and stared out at the dark. I wondered how far the lake was from the cabin. He came and stood next to me, offered me a glass of wine, and smiled that wonderful smile of his.

"It'll warm up in a minute," he said. "It won't take long."

To make conversation, I asked him about Tina.

"We're friends," he told me, which of course explained nothing.

I persisted: "But you did used to go out, didn't you?"

He shrugged and pointed out the window. In the darkness, I could just make out a slightly larger cabin, directly across the way.

"That's Tina's place," he said, and went on to explain that the two properties were owned by an old man who lived up the road. He and Tina each rented a cabin; it seemed to me that she had got the better deal.

"So you don't own this place," I said. "Tina said the two of you had bought the property together."

Michael smiled. "That's Tina. Always living life on a grand scale—in her head, anyway."

We talked about Mexico, where he'd been living, and Spain,

where he wanted to go. He wanted to travel and he wanted his mother to quit hassling him about school. Apart from that, he seemed remarkably unambitious. His needs were few, he said. Looking around the stark little cabin, I believed him.

That night we made love on a mattress in front of the fire. It should have been wonderful, being with him like that, but it was awkward and unsatisfying. In the middle of the night, I woke up disoriented, surrounded by a blackness that was almost absolute. The fire had gone out, as had the candles we'd lit, and the room was freezing. I felt exposed, helpless—wished I was back in the safety of my own bed. Michael was asleep next to me, flat on his back with one arm flung out to the side. To warm myself, I pressed against his naked body and he responded immediately. We made love again; this time, it was better.

When I think about Michael and me, and the short time we were together, I see us in that small cabin, the windows frosted against the night, and the books we were reading: *The Teachings of Don Juan, The Naked and the Dead, The Great Gatsby* (him); *The Golden Notebook, The Edible Woman, Sexual Politics* (me, along with, strangely enough, *Sons and Lovers* and *The Sun Also Rises*, too young to see the incongruity, thank heavens.) Reading, like writing, is a solitary act, yet we shared a companionable intimacy, lying in bed half-naked, propped up on our pillows, absorbed in our books. We could spend a whole evening this way, turning the pages at times in unison, scarcely speaking. There was something contained about that little place, like living inside one of those glass paperweights that snow when you shake them. I've never experienced that kind of perfect consonance, either before or since.

5

"ALEX! ARE YOU THERE? CALL ME."

My friend Liz would have you believe she's chronically pressed for time. And so she leaves these short, breathless messages, never saying hello, always hanging up before saying goodbye. It's a recent affectation, something she's adopted along with the spotless furniture and the weekly pedicures at *Maison de Chic.*

We've known each other since high school; she was my maid of honour when I married David, I flew back from Vancouver to be *her* maid of honour six months later. When, after years of putting up with extremely bad behaviour on his part, she finally split up with Bruno, I was immensely relieved but had the good sense to keep my feelings to myself. She has always bossed and mothered me and continues to do so, in spite of my letting her know I resent it. Still, she cares about me; I call her back.

"I was afraid something had happened to you," she says. "I couldn't imagine where you'd be, this time of the morning."

I tell her I was out walking the dog. And I had a call from David.

"How is he?"

"Fine, I guess. I hate talking to him on the phone, he never really sounds like himself. I told him about Joan."

"Of course—you had lunch together, didn't you? Did it go well?"

"Very well. I like her."

"I knew you would. Joan's quite rich, did you know that?"

"Really? I had no idea. Mind you, she has some great jewelry."

"She's a smart cookie. She invests in the stock market, buys real estate—all kinds of things. She hasn't had to work in years."

"We're having lunch again next Tuesday."

Now it's Liz's turn to sound surprised.

"Really? Why would you do that?"

"We've decided to get together once a week to talk about Tina. I think there's a lot she can tell me."

"Too much work, if you ask me. Driving all that way into town just to have lunch. I guess it's what you writers call research."

She's wrong, of course, research is scrolling through microfiche, shuffling pages of photocopied news clippings, dredging up conversations from the past.

Lunch is just lunch.

※ ※ ※

It was the house on Wilson Street that did us in, Michael and me, although it seemed a good idea at the time. We'd been living out at the lake, and it wasn't working out; I had early morning classes, which meant getting up when it was still dark out, scraping the frost off the windows of Michael's Renault and waiting a good fifteen minutes for the car to warm up. Not that it ever did. The drive into town was an endurance test—by the time Michael dropped me off at school I was numb with cold.

We could have moved in with my father; he had two furnished rooms in the basement and he lived less than ten minutes from the university. I didn't see why Michael would prefer an hour's drive in the cold to the comfort and convenience of staying at Dad's. Michael said he wouldn't feel comfortable sleeping with me in my father's house. He said it had to do with territory. And he liked the romance of staying out at the lake.

Eventually, the Renault broke down altogether and Michael couldn't afford to get it fixed. Now we had to stay in town—even *he* wasn't willing to hitchhike out to camp in the winter. We rented a room at Bunny's Motel and stayed there for a week. It cost six dollars a night, which was a lot of money back then, but I was so happy not to be making the journey out to the lake I offered to pay for it out of my student loan, while Michael looked for an apartment.

In the end it was Peter Canary who came up with the solution. Peter was a friend of Michael's, a good-looking guy whose only physical blemish was his teeth: they were a mess from all the speed he did. When he laughed he placed a hand over his mouth, not wanting to reveal the yellow, rotting stumps. He turned up at the motel one night and told us he'd found a place on Wilson Street—an old, two-storey house, unfurnished, with two bedrooms upstairs and three down, a couple of blocks from downtown. He couldn't afford it on his own and suggested the three of us move in together.

"We can have the main floor for sixty dollars a month," Peter said, "not including utilities. I'll pay twenty, you guys can pay forty and we'll split the cost of the cable."

It was the thought of cable that cinched it. Out at the lake we could only get the two local stations and as they were owned by the same company, there wasn't a lot of choice. We were missing episodes of *All My Children* and were stuck with reruns of *The Dating Game.*

"Who lives upstairs?" I wanted to know.

"Some old guy lives in one of the rooms. The landlord says he's never around. And the other room is empty."

Michael asked about furniture and Peter said we could pick up stuff second-hand from the Sally Ann.

"My sister will give us a fridge," he said. "She's renting a furnished place now and says she doesn't need it."

From the moment we moved in, I knew it was a mistake. There was an unhappy feeling about the house, as if someone had died there. The three of us spent less time there than we'd expected. Michael, who was working part-time at the shipyard, got into the habit of getting up with me in the morning and accompanying me to class, just to get out of the house.

Still, there were some good times. Nights when we sat around on cushions on the living room floor, eating spaghetti and listening to Jimi Hendrix and the Stones. Drinking wine, smoking dope, practising chords on Michael's guitar. Having a whole house practically to ourselves meant we could play our music as loudly as we wanted. There was nobody to tell us to keep the noise down for God's sake, who the hell do you think you are?

The old guy who lived upstairs slept all day and left his room early in the evening to go drink at the Lakefront Hotel. He wasn't ancient, no older than my father, and whenever our paths crossed I spoke to him politely because he was the father of somebody, somebody's husband. He didn't seem to care how much noise we made. He never banged on the floor to get us to shut up, never came downstairs to tell us we were an inconsiderate bunch of hooligans, disturbing an old man's sleep. He came and went and left us alone. Most of the time, I'm sure he didn't even notice us.

There was a time when Wilson Street was populated by Italian and Ukrainian immigrants who tended vegetable gardens in their backyards and raised large, noisy, loving families. But those people had died or moved away. By the time we moved in, the street was full of transients with a few fearful elderly couples and some solitary men who'd spent their working lives in the bush or on the railroad and now lived alone in dreary single rooms, drinking beer and watching television. It was not the kind of street where you particularly wanted to get to know your neighbours. A house right on the corner was owned by the Satan's Choice, and on warm nights motorcycles filled the front yard and the bikers spilled out on to the steps, noisy and just a little bit scary. I always hurried past that house when I left for school in the morning; even with the curtains drawn it made me uneasy.

We'd been living in the Wilson Street house for about two months when spring finally came and Peter and Michael went smelting. They offered to take me with them, but I knew they wanted to go on their own. They left on a Saturday morning just before daybreak and were gone the whole day, right until dark. When they came back with their catch they were tired and messy and just a little drunk. I could see what a good time they'd had together and it made me a little envious, so I offered to do the cooking, even though I'd never cooked fresh fish in my life. I just wanted to have a part in the ritual.

Peter said he'd clean them for me first, and he did so while Michael went out to buy wine. I watched as he laid a sheet of newspaper on the kitchen counter and spread each small fish out on the paper, made a slice right down the belly, took hold of the inner gills, and pulled. The insides came out in one swift, easy motion; he threw them into a bucket on the floor and dropped the fish, head and tail intact, into the sink. He made it look easy but when I tried, I made a mess of it. It made me queasy to touch the cold, slippery skin and I couldn't seem to get a proper hold on it. The fish slipped out of my hands altogether and fell on the floor. Peter laughed and picked it up and called me a city girl, which of course I was.

I made a better job of cooking them. I dipped each fish into a mixture of flour and cornmeal after sprinkling them first with lemon juice. Then I cooked them, three or four at a time, in melted butter in a pan on the stove. I cooked more than we could possibly eat, and we still had dozens left over. These we cleaned and wrapped in plastic bags and stuffed into the freezer. Peter said we'd have fresh frozen fish all summer. I made a salad and Michael came back with two kinds of wine—Liebfraumilch and something red and musky—and we took our plates into the living room and ate, since we didn't own a table.

I have it in my head that when we finished the smelts, when none of us could bear to look another fish in the eye, Peter brought out his "special stash" and rolled us a couple of joints. Michael had a couple of tokes, then said he was tired and was going to bed. He kissed me, smelling of fish and cigarettes, and left the room. Peter and I sprawled out on the living room rug, passing a joint between us. We'd had too much wine and food, and Peter's dope was very strong.

We didn't actually make love; I don't think we were capable of it that night. We just sort of rolled around together on the carpet, necking in a lazy, haphazard fashion, and stopping now and then to roll another joint. It was silly and harmless. Only someone as rigid as Michael was would have seen it as a betrayal. When I finally came to bed, he was lying on his side, facing the wall, pretending to be asleep. As I pulled back the covers and got in beside him, he turned and looked at me. And I knew he had been awake the whole time.

"Michael?"

He just looked at me.

I couldn't begin to think what to say. I was stoned and tired. All I really wanted to do was to crawl into bed and go to sleep.

"Had a nice time?"

Before I could answer, he turned back and faced the wall

again. I reached out and touched his back, but he didn't respond. I was too tired to stay awake any longer.

For almost a week Michael refused to speak to me. He stayed in bed when I left the house in the morning and was gone when I came back at suppertime. When we were in the house together, he would ignore me altogether. When he absolutely had to speak to me, he would do it in a deliberately casual tone, barely concealing his anger.

Just when I thought I couldn't bear it any more, he started talking to me again and behaved as if nothing had come between us. I was relieved until I realized that it was only an act. He was still angry with me but had decided to pretend to forgive me. At night, though, it was obvious that we were still in trouble. He kept as far away from me as possible when we were in bed and would not make love to me. Once, overcoming my shyness about these things, I asked him if he wanted to have sex.

"No, thank you," he said, as if I'd been offering him a cup of tea. "I don't think we'll be doing that again."

The feeling in the house got worse. The walls heaved with a kind of silent reproach, the windows were dark and hostile. A crew of workmen came and tore down the house across the street. We now had a clear view of an old, derelict warehouse, one street over. It had been a factory storehouse at one time, but it was obvious now that it was used as a brothel. At night when Michael and Peter were out, I sat alone in the dark and looked out at that building. Sometimes its inhabitants left their lights on and undressed in front of the window. It might have been titillating if it hadn't been so depressing.

It was right about then that a couple moved into the empty room upstairs. I only saw them once or twice, but I often heard them: their room was directly above our bedroom. They were very young, younger than us, and she was pregnant. They looked frightened and unhappy. They always came in around ten at night and left first thing in the morning.

One night when Michael was out, I went to bed early and awoke around midnight. Something had woken me up; it was the girl upstairs, crying. She cried for a very long time, horrible, penetrating sobs that sounded as if they were being wrenched from deep within her. I didn't move, I hardly dared to breathe, I just lay there listening to her cry. Eventually, after I don't know how long—an hour, maybe not quite that long—the crying stopped and it was very quiet. They must have fallen asleep. I lay awake for some time after that and made up my mind I would leave the very next day; I wouldn't stay one minute longer in this terribly sad, old building. And then in the morning I lost my nerve—I didn't go.

They did, however. Whatever the crying was about that night, I guess it settled something. Early in the morning I heard them clatter down the front staircase and head out the door. They never came back.

When I realized they were gone for good, I was glad. This was a terrible place to start a family, an awful place to be pregnant and poor. Maybe they'd go back to her family, or his. Maybe they'd move out to the coast. Whatever they did, it would have to be better than staying in this dismal house where nobody seemed to be happy.

In the end, it took a fire to get us out. It started in an upstairs room late at night. One of the bikers from the house on the corner pounded on our door and shouted to wake us up. Half asleep, I grabbed the stereo, Michael gathered up a stack of record albums, I heard Peter call out from the kitchen, "The dope—where'd we put the dope?" The three of us stood outside in the dark, clutching our possessions, while the firemen put out the smoke and flames. The fire created a temporary kinship with our neighbours: a handful of them stood around and talked to us for the first time, and shared stories of household disasters of their own.

It was one of them who asked about the old guy who lived upstairs. In all the confusion, Michael and Peter and I had completely forgotten we had a roommate. I ran over to one of the firemen and told them there was an old man who lived in the upstairs bedroom. He must be still in there, I said, he must be trapped. The firemen, who had been relatively relaxed up to this point, immediately switched into high gear. They barked orders to each other and one of them entered the smoke-filled house and rushed up the stairs. Which was when the old guy came ambling up the street towards us, a little unsteady on his feet.

"Where were you?" Michael asked.

The old guy pointed back down the street, towards the waterfront hotel on the corner.

"Fell asleep," he said in a soft, shaky voice. He was tiny and shrunken and looked as though he might fall over any moment. "Woke up, place was full of smoke. So I got the hell outta there."

He stared at what was left of our home and slowly shook his head, as if he couldn't quite believe it.

"Guess I dropped my smoke," he said, and he smiled at me, like a little kid admitting he'd picked the crabapples off the neighbour's tree.

And that was the end of it. Michael and I moved into my father's house; Peter moved in with his sister and her kids. As for the old guy, I guess he went back to the hotel. A few days later, Michael moved out on his own. I didn't see him again for almost six years.

6

As planned, Joan and I meet for lunch again the following Tuesday. We decide to forego the soup in favour of the house special—a large chef's salad with strips of barbecued chicken. Joan wants to know if the chicken can be replaced with stir-fried tofu, and when the waitress appears uncertain, she opts instead for a plain salad, no extras.

After the waitress leaves, Joan explains she's been a vegetarian for the past ten years—since being diagnosed with breast cancer.

"I read everything written on the subject. And I kept coming across all these studies that were done about cancer in mice—all the stuff they've done over the years to get laboratory mice to develop cancer. Really awful things, like taking away their babies, exposing them to high levels of noise and bright lights, keeping them trapped in little cages and giving them constant electric shocks. After a while, reading about this, I began to wonder why we thought we had the right to do that to another of God's creatures? And if we shouldn't be shocking them and taking away their babies, then maybe we shouldn't be eating them either. Animals, I mean, not mice. So I went vegetarian, and the cancer went away and never came back, touch wood."

"Was it being vegetarian that did it?" I'm wondering if it's too late to change my order.

"It's hard to say. The chemo helped, I'm sure. And I stopped smoking. The one thing I wouldn't give up was wine."

"Wine's good for you, isn't that what they say? Good for the heart."

Joan raises her glass and proposes a toast:

"Drink thy wine with a merry heart, for God now accepteth thy works. Ecclesiastes, chapter nine, verse seven."

Solemnly, we clink our classes together and drink.

"I'm impressed," I tell her. "I thought it was only Baptists who could recite scripture."

"I grew up Presbyterian," she says. "On my mother's side, that is. Jewish on my father's. Non-practising. The only thing they ever agreed on was the Old Testament. Now you know everything there is to know about me—I'm a Jewish-Presbyterian cancer survivor who grew up on the wrong side of the tracks."

"That's it?"

"Isn't that enough?" she laughs.

The waitress appears with our salads, and I am distracted by the sheer size of the servings. An entire head of Boston lettuce gave its life for my portion alone, while Joan's plate is a cornucopia of cucumber and tomatoes, to make up for the absent chicken. I pick up my fork, resolved to at least try to make a dent in my allotment.

"This is obscene," Joan says. "It's vegetable pornography."

She spears a wedge of tomato with her fork and sighs.

"I'll never finish this. I'm beaten before I begin."

Putting her fork down, she pushes her plate to one side and confides that she's not particularly hungry.

"Let's just talk," she says. "Or rather, I'll talk—you eat. Where should we start?"

"Tell me about Conrad. What was he like?"

"Well, first of all, he was gorgeous, in a bad-boy kind of way. When I was eleven I had an intense crush on him. I was friends with his sister, Nadine, and I used to bug her to invite me over to her house after school. But he was hardly ever there. Anyway, I don't think I was Conrad's type."

"They were from Germany, right? It says something about that in his obit."

They came to Canada, Joan says, after the separation of East and West Germany, when the Enemy Alien Protection Act was lifted. None of them spoke English, not Rudy, his father, or Klara, his mother, and the money was all spent getting here.

"His dad got hired on at the coal yards, but they were dirt poor. That first winter they didn't even have a proper place to live in. They lived in a garage—no heating, no insulation—and there were rats, because they were right down by the tracks. The old man who rented out the place was a bastard. He knew no regular Canadian would have stayed in a one-room shack in a backyard filled with junk. The place was barely fit for chickens, but I guess the Schaeffers were just grateful to be out of Germany. Poor, ignorant DPs, that's what they were."

The following winter was cold too, but by then the Schaeffers had found better accommodation, a proper house two streets over. It wasn't a palace, by any means, but it wasn't a garage, either. And that's where Conrad grew up.

"You have to understand," Joan tells me, frowning into her wineglass, "being raised in that kind of neighbourhood does things to you. I'm not making excuses for Conrad—or for myself—but it's a long way from the suburbs, that's for sure."

Joan tells me that, as long as she can remember, Conrad had a reputation as a tough guy. First day of school, he'd go up to the biggest guy in the playground and pick a fight. The bigger kid would laugh it off: what was he going to prove by squashing this little punk like a bug? It was too easy to even be interesting. But Conrad would persist, harass the guy, call him names, call his mother names, until finally, out of exasperation, the bigger kid would agree to meet him at the far end of the schoolyard, at the end of the day. They'd meet up, they'd fight, and Conrad would get the crap beaten out of him. End of story.

Except that it wasn't. Conrad wouldn't give up, wouldn't concede defeat, would keep kicking and punching and rolling around in the dirt as long as he could physically move. And then, the very next day, he'd do it all over again. Go up to the bigger guy, pick another fight, goad him into repeating the whole pathetic farce. Eventually, the other guy would simply refuse to fight, refuse to be goaded, because Conrad was obviously nuts—he didn't know when he was beat, there was just no stopping him. At which point Conrad would turn his attentions to the next big guy and goad him into fighting and—well, you get the picture. Soon Conrad's prowess as a fighter was legendary: the bigger guys left him alone; the kids his own age paid him due respect.

None of this got him very far with his teachers, of course, but Conrad never cared about school. For one thing, he couldn't concentrate; he had too much energy to sit still very long.

"He was probably bored," Joan says. "I mean, one thing about Conrad, he wasn't stupid. But he had all this energy and he just kept getting into trouble. The teachers kept kicking him out of class, and his mother kept bringing him back. He just didn't seem to be able to control himself."

Once, when Joan was visiting Conrad's sister, she saw a copy of *The Catcher in the Rye*. She was impressed in spite of herself when Nadine told her Conrad was reading it. Other books appeared with regularity: *For Whom the Bell Tolls, The Maltese Falcon, A Tale of Two Cities*. When he was home—and much of the time he wasn't—Conrad was always reading. And listening to music.

"What about the Elvis thing?" I want to know. "When did he get started on that?"

"I think it was right after his father died," Joan says. "That movie came out, *G.I. Blues*. Conrad must've seen it a dozen times; he could recite whole scenes by heart. He started talking like Elvis and wearing his hair like him. He told Nadine that when he was sixteen he was going to take off to the States and join the army, just like Elvis. He was nuts about the guy."

"Did he do it?"

Joan shakes her head. "He got into a fight with a guy down at the pool hall, smashed him with a pool cue or something. Anyway, he got sent to the juvenile detention centre for six months. When he came out he was still crazy about Elvis, but I don't remember him talking about the army after that."

Conrad had another connection with Elvis, Joan says—they were both devoted to their mothers.

"He was the prince of the family," she says. "He got the most food, the second helping of pie. Klara was always ironing his shirts and picking up after him, and if she was too busy, she made his sisters do it instead. I used to ask Nadine why she didn't just tell Conrad to shove it, and she said that's the way it was in the old country: the women did all the work and the men sat around getting waited on, hand and foot. She really didn't seem to mind."

After high school, Joan moved out of the neighbourhood, but she ran into Conrad occasionally. He had enlisted half the city in something called the Purple Gang; his little brother, Leo, was their mascot.

"They were a notorious gang in Chicago or New York apparently," Joan says, "and Elvis sang about them in 'Jailhouse Rock': 'The whole rhythm section was the Purple Gang, / Let's rock, everybody let's rock.' It was sort of an in joke, I guess— Conrad or Herbie would walk into a bar and they'd have their index finger up in the air as a kind of salute."

"The Purple Gang. I never knew what that meant."

"Me neither. But it just goes to show you, he was really into Elvis. If you ever talk to his family, you'll get to meet Leo. He has Down's Syndrome, and he still, after all these years, carries on the tradition. He's been to Graceland, does all the moves—the whole thing."

Joan tops up our wineglasses.

"Actually," she says, "you know who you should talk to? Vicky Ternetti."

It takes me a moment to recognize the name.

"Vicky Ternetti. You must remember her. Dark hair, great figure. She was a cocktail waitress, remember? I think she worked at The Flame."

"Oh, my God. Is she still alive?"

"She's alive, all right," Joan says. "She has to be seventy if she's a day and she looks terrific. She could tell you a lot about Conrad—she was crazy about the guy." According to Joan, Vicky lived with Conrad for three or four years, before he met Tina. She was older than him, by fifteen or twenty years, but she adored him. The story goes, Joan says, that the Christmas after he died, Vicky dragged a fully decorated tree out to the cemetery, and spent the night at Conrad's grave, drinking tequila and singing carols.

"Every year, on the anniversary of his death, she puts one of those In Memoriam notices in the newspaper. She's always said he died in her arms, although there are so many stories out there about the guy, it's hard to separate fiction from fact. But I do think you should give her a call."

7

CONSIDERING THE LIFE SHE'S LED, THE WOMAN WHO
answers the doorbell looks pretty damn good. She's thin as a
rake, and her makeup is perfect, although a little on the heavy
side for a senior citizen. Seems to me Vicky Ternetti's a walking
advertisement for the benefits of good bones and amphetamines.

"I don't have a lot of time," she says. "Will this take long?"

"No, no," I assure her. "A half-hour, forty-five minutes at
the most."

"It was all so long ago," she says. "I'm not sure I can help
you."

She nods for me to come in, then shuts the door immediately behind me and locks it. Outside the day is cold but bright,
a typical northern fall morning; inside, with the curtains
drawn, there's a dusty darkness, the way funeral parlours used
to be before they discovered marketing. She leads me through
a tiny living room, past a picture of the Sacred Heart, several
crucifixes, and a painting of the Last Supper. A half-dozen
framed photographs are clustered on top of the television set,
which is turned on with the sound muted, and several more
pictures are ranged along the kitchen window. There's one of a
good-looking young man holding a guitar. I think it might be
Conrad, but don't like to ask.

The kitchen, at least, is bright, thanks to the sun streaming
in through the window, which looks out on to the harbour and
the Sleeping Giant in the distance. I can imagine that this
room, too, will slip into darkness in the late afternoon, as the
sun makes its way westward.

Vicky invites me to sit down, then perches on a stool across from me and pulls a pack of cigarettes out of the side pocket of her pants. Her hands are shaking, just a little, which might be old age, or the effects of a thirty-year diet of speed.

When I mention Conrad's name, she purses her lips and studies me, her dark eyes searching my face for clues.

"It was a long time ago," she repeats, and I wonder if she is going to refuse to talk about him after all. I'm prepared for that; I am also prepared to sit there and wait, if she'll let me.

Lighting her cigarette, she drags deeply on it, as if she's hungry for more than smoke. And then she appears to make up her mind.

"He was a very beautiful young man," she begins, like she's reciting an old, well-known story. "You need to understand that. A lot of men are attractive, but Conrad was beautiful. And physically, he was strong. He was always getting into fights—he worked out, lifted weights and all that, and he had studied karate. But mentally, he was weak."

Quickly, she adds that by "mentally weak" she doesn't mean he was stupid. She means he was easily dominated by women; he let himself be controlled by them. Because of his mother, I ask?

Vicky shrugs. "Who knows? That's for the shrinks to figure out. All I know is the danger was always there with Conrad, there was always the chance he'd get caught up with some woman who'd hurt him. And that's what happened, wasn't it? He met Tina and she got him hooked on pills. She was stronger than he was, and it wasn't a good kind of strength. I saw it happening, I tried to tell him, but it was too late. He wasn't listening."

She takes another drag on her cigarette. I ask her why she and Conrad broke up.

Margie Taylor

"We had a fight," she says, shaking her head at the foolishness of it all. "Something stupid, I can't even tell you what we fought about. Nothing important. But I got mad and kicked him out. Well, for heavens sake, I'd kicked him out dozens of times before. He was always doing something to make me mad."

She smiles, and I wonder if that was part of the attraction—he was a naughty little boy who liked to be mothered.

"So he goes off to the lake, and stays with Tina," she says. "It was the camp, really, that he liked. He liked to get away like that, with nobody around to bug him. And, of course, she had the drugs."

In her opinion, Conrad was not in love with Tina and in time he would have left her. Tina controlled his drug supply, and as long as that was important to Conrad, he'd stay with her.

"He was crazy about me," Vicky says. "He used to say I looked like Priscilla. Elvis's wife, you know? He liked me to wear my hair up and put on lots of makeup. He'd say, 'Baby, you look just like Priscilla.' That was really the highest compliment he could give a woman, that she looked like Elvis's wife."

When she heard the news on the radio that Elvis had died—"They said it was a heart attack, but of course, we all knew it was drugs"—she immediately thought of Conrad. Elvis was his hero; he was more than a fan—he had a *connection* with the singer, you know? So she called him. He came over, and they held each other. He told Vicky that this was worse than when Buddy Holly died, worse even than when Kennedy got shot. Elvis was the King, and no one would ever be able to take his place.

"The papers were full of it," Vicky says, "and Conrad was saving all the news stories. He asked me to clip them for him, whenever I saw anything, *anything* about Elvis's death. He said he was putting together a scrapbook—he was planning to write a book about Elvis. He didn't, though. He didn't have time."

Conrad went back out to his camp on Lake Superior, the one he'd bought a few months earlier. He was supposed to be out there working on it, fixing it up to be lived in. Tina was with him when he collapsed. When they got him to the hospital, it turned out he'd taken a bunch of pills and his heart had just stopped.

The doctors kept him there overnight, and the following morning he turned up again at Vicky's place. She had a bottle of tequila in the cupboard; the two of them started drinking. When the booze was gone, Vicky went upstairs to bed and Conrad called a cab. She thinks he may have gone over to his mother's place then, but she's not sure.

"I know where he ended up, though," Vicky says. "At the Avenue Hotel, on Bay Street. His friends were all there— Herbie Sunderland was with him. You remember Herbie?"

"I know the name," I tell her. "I never actually met him."

When I was growing up, Herbie Sunderland was our local Al Capone. One of those guys you saw around all the time, getting in trouble with the cops, beating people up. He was only a few years older than me, but he was from another era. When we were younger we called them "greasers," tough guys who bypassed the peace and love generation and headed right into jail.

"Too bad he's dead," Vicky says. "Herbie could have told you a lot about that night."

Conrad and Herbie and a bunch of the guys were drinking tequila, she says, and Conrad was popping pills. It's like he was crazy, like he was angry he hadn't died the night before.

Sometime before midnight somebody called a cab for him, and the driver dropped him off at Vicky's front door. She could see right away that he was in a bad way. He was drunk, but he was drugged as well. That was what bothered her; she'd seen him drunk many times, but she'd never seen him so completely disoriented.

She offered to make him something to eat and he asked for fish.

"Our Lord ate fish at the Last Supper," he said.

So she fried up some pickerel she had in the fridge, sat him down at the kitchen table and watched him while he ate. When he was finished he got up and went into the living room, put a record of Elvis hymns on the stereo.

A small, gold cross hangs from a chain around her throat; she lifts it towards me, holds it up for me to see.

"Conrad wore this all the time," she says. "He never took it off. But that night he took it off and put it around my neck. 'You keep this, Vicky,' he told me. 'Don't ever take it off.' Then he went and sat down on the couch and I sat on the floor in front of him."

She stops now, waits for me to ask what happened next.

"He was very quiet," she says. "We were listening to the music, just sitting there, not saying anything, and something made me turn around to look at him. And he was dead."

She called an ambulance, and they took him to the hospital, but he was dead on arrival. Died there, just like that, on Vicky's couch.

Her story told, she seems anxious to have me leave. She has errands to do, she says, glancing at the clock on the wall. Her grandson is coming for dinner, she has to pick some things up at the store. When I take her hand to say goodbye, I can feel the delicate bones, like thin sticks encased in velvet.

"He was beautiful, you know," she reminds me, "and he was the love of my life." Then she pulls away and shuts the door quickly, as if she's unwilling to put herself on display for the neighbours.

8

THE SNOW BEGINS TO FALL JUST AFTER DARK. SOFTLY, at first, a whisper of icy crystals, like a stranger tossing a handful of sand at the windowpane. Around midnight the wind wakes me from a dream in which a bearded man has me pinned against the mattress and is tying my hands and feet to the bedstead. I discover the dog asleep on the bed, spread out across my lower legs and snoring.

With some difficulty, I pull my feet out from under him, turn over and fall back asleep. By morning, the snow is still falling, thicker now than during the night. Great, whirling clumps of snow beat against the glass. Trying to see outside is like peering into extinction. The surrounding trees, the lake, everything has been obliterated by a dense whiteness.

I don't realize the power's gone off until I check the clock in the kitchen: the digital dial is blinking 12:00, and the overhead light doesn't come on when I flick the switch.

I pick up the phone, and the line is dead. Sometime during the night the wind must have taken down a telephone pole or two; who knows how long it'll take them to fix it? The battery-operated radio works, and I rotate the dial until I locate the following conversation, carried out with the usual morning radio jokiness that makes you want to reach right through the speaker and strangle the DJ:

"So how bad is it out there, Gord?"

"Pretty bad, Matt. Looks like we're in for a real blizzard. We're expecting up to thirty centimetres of snow by tomorrow afternoon, and there's a wind chill factor right now of minus thirty."

This is said in a tone of such upbeat optimism that you'd think one of them had just won the lottery.

"Is this the beginning of El Niño, Gord?"

"Hard to say, Matt. It's a little early for El Niño. Let's just say it's an early winter storm."

"A good day to stay indoors and listen to the radio, Gordo."

"You got it, fella. I wouldn't take my dog out in this."

I switch off the radio and tell myself there's nothing to panic about. There's food and firewood and once the weather clears they'll get the phone lines operating and the power back on. First priority, build up the fire in the cast-iron stove and get some coffee made. Nobody can be expected to face the storm of the decade without caffeine.

Except that there is the matter of the dog. I crouch down in order to look him directly in the eyes, and explain that right now is not a good time to be heading outside.

The dog whimpers and shifts on his haunches. Taking his muzzle in my hands, I speak very slowly and distinctly.

"Jake, we are not going out. You heard the weather guy. He said he wouldn't take his dog out on a day like this. You're a dog—I'm not taking you out."

The whimper becomes a whine, which leads to a series of whines, which will eventually, I know, evolve into yelps. I offer him a biscuit, which he ignores. Storm or no storm, this dog has to do his business. I'll have to let him out.

"Hang on, boy," I tell him, "let me get some clothes on."

I'll have to wear something warmer than the light fall jacket I've been trotting around in since I got here. The Hendersons, Arizona-bound, have left behind a closet full of winter wear—jackets, coats, parkas, toques. I grab what looks like the warmest one and try it on for size: a little big, it probably belongs to Harry. But it's down-filled and warm.

Margie Taylor

By the time I've zipped up the parka and pulled on my boots, the dog has worked himself into an anxious frenzy. While I'm searching for his leash—which hasn't been used since the first week we were here—he's pawing at the door, whining fretfully, clearly in some distress. I can't find the leash, and he can't wait; I decide to let him out just for a minute. He won't go far, I reason, opening the door. It's freezing out. He'll do his business and scamper right back inside.

I open the door and the dog dashes past me out into the snowy vortex. And disappears.

※ ※ ※

When David and I were first married, we lived in London for a year while he completed his Ph.D. We had a flat in Notting Hill, and all I remember about that cold, cramped little place was that it was up four flights of stairs, and we shared the bath with an Australian architecture student who consistently left a dirty yellow ring in the tub.

Every morning, David walked down the stairs to the street, hopped on the bus to the tube station, and took the underground to the British Museum. And I spent the day getting lost.

For the entire time we lived there, I managed to get lost briefly each and every day. Eventually, I learned that if I was coming out of a building and all my instincts told me to turn right, then the correct way to proceed was to the left.

My sense of direction has not improved with age: I am not a person who should ever, under any circumstances, venture out into a blinding northern Ontario storm.

For half a minute I stand with the door halfway open and wait, certain that the dog will reappear any minute, come bounding up the steps, shaking the snow from his sleek black coat, leaving wet footprints all over the kitchen floor.

"Jake? Come on, boy! Jake!"

No response. I continue calling into the wind, but I'd need a megaphone to make myself heard over the racket nature is creating. The dog would have to be less than twenty feet from the house to hear me, and I'm pretty sure he's not.

I shut the door and try to think. My options, as I see them, are to wait inside for the dog to return, which good sense tells me he must, eventually; or head out into the storm to look for him. He can't have gone far and will probably have left tracks in the snow. Dogs, even old ones, have a better sense of direction than most humans. He'll find his way back. And yet.

The longer I wait, the further away, the more lost he could be. I make up my mind to go looking for him, but I won't go far. I'll keep the cabin in sight, give myself twenty minutes at most, and if I can't find him I'll come back and wait it out. I find gloves and a scarf and, at the bottom of the closet, the dog's leash. Opening the door, it seems to me that the wind is blowing even harder than it was. I pause on the steps, uncertain if I should proceed. I call his name again, but no reassuring black shape bounds towards me. I decide to head down to the lake.

Under normal circumstances, this is the way he would go, but today I'm handicapped by the fact that I can't see the lake, can't see more than a few feet in front of me. I walk blindly in the direction of the water, calling constantly:

"Jake! Here, boy! Come on, Jake, come here!"

The ground gives suddenly beneath my feet and I stumble and slip, regaining my balance with difficulty. I've reached the water's edge, where the grassy verge gives way to rocks and driftwood and slopes directly to the shoreline. It's impossible to see anything of the lake itself except for the waves right at my feet, but the dog, I know, would not go further. I walk up and down the beach, sliding on snow-covered rocks. So much snow has fallen—continues to fall—that there's almost no distinction between land and water. Behind me, when I turn to look, the cabin has disappeared into the whitened landscape. I know where it *should* be, but I can't see it.

It's at this point that the first law of survival kicks in: every man for himself. The dog has a thick coat of fur, a good sense of smell, and the instinct to find his way back. He may have already found his way back, be waiting to be let in at the front door. I abandon the search and make my way up the sloping yard, towards the cabin, turning my face away from the full force of the wind.

At the top of the slope I stumble against something hard and out-of-place. It's the stump of a large tree. To the best of my knowledge, the Hendersons' yard contains no stumps of any size.

I've come too far along the beach; the cabin is obviously further back. If that's the case, though, I should be on the driveway, the long dirt road that leads up to the main beach. And surely there are no large tree stumps in the middle of the road. I turn a little to the left, take a few more steps, and I'm at the edge of a thicket, low, snow-covered bushes leading into the woods; I've travelled even further along the beach than I thought. This strip of bush, however, can't be more than a few yards thick—the road has to be just beyond it.

I've been out for maybe ten minutes at the most, and my cheeks are numb from the cold. My forehead is beginning to ache and my chin is wet from the condensation caused by the wet wool scarf against my skin. All I want to do now is find the road and get back to the cabin. I'll worry about the dog later.

Pressing further through the bushes and trees, ducking to avoid being slapped in the face by evergreen branches, I expect

*dis*placed PERSONS

at any minute to step out of the trees and on to the road. The problem is, with the snow incessantly swirling around me and showing no signs of letting up, I've lost my bearings. I can't tell if I'm heading north, which is where the road should be, or east, which will keep me struggling through the bush. I'd turn and head back the way I came, if I could be sure which way was back. In trying to make a path through the trees, I've zig-zagged all over the place. And my heart is pounding so furiously it hurts to breathe.

Hug a tree, that's what they tell you. Stay put, wait it out. Don't keep moving. But I'm freezing, I'm not dressed for staying out here for much longer. My hands, in particular, are getting cold. I should've worn mitts, these gloves are useless.

All at once I'm overtaken by an overwhelming urge to run. I have no idea where I am, or even in which direction I'm facing, but my instinct tells me if I want to get out of this mess, I have to run like hell. Although logic says running is the last thing I should be doing, my feet are on automatic pilot: I am racing through the bush, weaving my way through the slender trees that appear, ghostlike, out of nowhere—slipping and stumbling and ducking the low-hanging, snow-laden branches. An unseen log trips me up, and I fall forward into a bush, face first.

I pull myself up and check the damage—a few scratches, most likely, nothing else. My pride is hurt more than anything else. All the things I've done wrong this morning: shouldn't have let the dog out without a leash, shouldn't have come out myself, if I was going to come out I should have tied a rope or something to the door handle to lead me back, I should have brought a compass, and I should have stayed out in the open. That's a lot of mistakes for one person to make. One or two of them would be enough to get a person in trouble; if I freeze to death out here in the middle of the bush, it will be my own fault.

Margie Taylor

The scarf has become loose, exposing my chin to the wind and snow. I knot it more tightly, then notice there's a drop of blood on my gloves—my chin is bleeding. I reach into the deep pockets of the parka to search for a Kleenex, and encounter something small and hard at the very bottom of the right pocket.

At first, I think it's some kind of candy. God knows how long it's been there, probably since the last time the parka was worn, which would be six months ago at least. I pull it out of my pocket and see that it's not a candy—it's red and made of plastic and it's attached to a cord. It's a whistle.

Raising it to my shivering lips, I give it a speculative blow. The sound it emits is faint, as if it's rusty from disuse. I take a deep breath and give it a good, hard blow. The whistle responds with a sharp, piercing note that resonates through the clamour of the storm, loud enough to be heard by the neighbours, if there were any. I blow it again and again, because it feels comforting to have something to do; I'm not expecting a response.

I'm about to put the whistle back in the jacket pocket when I hear something. It might be the wind, but it sounds like a dog barking. I blow the whistle again, just once, and the bark answers. It seems as if it's come from behind me. I turn around, take a few tentative steps and blow the whistle again. Again, the answering bark, as clear and immediate as an echo. For the next few minutes I push through the bushes, alternately blowing the whistle and waiting for the bark. By now I'm sure it's Jake, although I can't see him and have no idea where exactly he is. The barking is louder now, and more frequent. The dog is barking almost continuously, as if he, too, is excited.

When I finally push my way out of the trees, I'm elated to the point of bursting. I may be lost, but I'm out of the woods. A few more steps in the direction of the barking and I stumble against something hard, a three-foot-high pile of snow that appears to be covering something made of cement. I brush away some of the snow and expose a large, concrete bowl. The bird bath. I'm in the Hendersons' backyard, less than twenty feet from the cabin.

The dog bounds towards me, yelping ecstatically. Frozen to the marrow though I am, I kneel down and give him a hug. He covers my face with joyous licks, but I'm the one who should be grateful. To him and to Harry Henderson, whom I have never met, for leaving his whistle in his jacket pocket.

9

THE STORM CONTINUES FOR THE REST OF THE DAY. Thanks to the battery in my laptop and the propane lantern, I can work and read. The fire in the stove keeps the place warm. Cooking is slightly more challenging. Briefly, I consider trying to make a pot of stew on top of the wood stove, but it seems like too much work. In the end I heat water in a saucepan and make Kraft Dinner.

There's something about being trapped inside like this that makes me ravenous; I could eat a horse—a small one, anyway. Too impatient to set a place for myself at the table, I stand at the stove and eat the macaroni directly out of the pot—something I've chastised Adam for doing at least a dozen times in the past. As I scrape the last of the noodles from the bottom of the saucepan, it suddenly occurs to me that there are Girl Guide cookies in the trunk of the car. A clutch of small girls in uniform descended on me during one of my forays into town; they brought back memories of Kate at that age and I bought six boxes.

I'll never eat these, I thought, and left them in the car. Now, though, the craving for chocolate mint is battling my fear of getting lost, and the craving is winning. Wrapped up in Harry's jacket, I retrieve a flashlight from a kitchen drawer and very carefully step outside. There's an outdoor plug next to the door, at the same level as the front step. I bend down, fumble around in the snow until I find what I'm looking for. Buried in two feet of snow is the long yellow extension cord that leads to the heater of my car, parked up on the road. As long as I keep hold of this cord, and it doesn't come unplugged, I can't get lost. For good measure, I give it a tug; it stays plugged in.

And so, very slowly, keeping the cord in one hand and the flashlight in the other, I plod through the snow to the large, snow-covered heap that is my vehicle. Brushing away the snow, I locate the door handle and give it a pull. The door stays shut— frozen, no doubt. Exasperated, I struggle with it for a moment and am about to give up when, miraculously, the door suddenly swings open.

With the help of the flashlight, I spring the trunk lock open, locate the cookies, and return slowly but triumphantly to the cabin. The warmth and security of the place is doubly comforting after this second foray into the storm; I have shelter and I have cookies. And I have a battery-powered vibrator. I have everything I need.

✕ ✕ ✕

Tina was the first woman I knew who owned a vibrator and used it regularly. She showed it to me years ago, in my father's basement. She had a name for it: "Oscar." It was a Panabrator, with a foot-long handle and a big, round, vibrating head. When she plugged it in and switched it on, it sounded like a buzz saw.

"He's a little noisy," Tina admitted over the din. "But he's wonderful. Show me yours."

When I told her I didn't own one, she was surprised.

"I thought you were a feminist."

I didn't get the connection; she said it was about being sexually independent, not relying on a man to make you come.

"Isn't that what women's lib is all about?"

I said I didn't trust the technology: I wasn't comfortable holding something electrical against my crotch.

She smiled. "So you're a Luddite as well," she said. "I think

66

that's kind of sweet. But really, Alex, you don't know what you're missing."

It was June 1972, a few months after Michael and I broke up, and I had run into her downtown on a hot Saturday afternoon. I was pleased but a little taken aback that she seemed so happy to see me. She said she'd had a fight with her landlord and had been kicked out of her apartment. She couldn't move out to her place on the lake because she'd sublet it for the summer. Without giving it much thought, I suggested she come stay at my father's place. There were two bedrooms in the basement; I was living in one of them, the other had been recently vacated.

Tina jumped at the offer and said she'd move in tomorrow, if that was all right. Just for a couple of months, she told me: "Tell your dad not to expect me to stay very long. I'll be going back out to camp at the end of August when my tenants move out."

She liked the sound of the word "tenants," you could tell. It had a businesslike ring about it, even though you knew the tenants were most likely summer session students who were behind with the rent and would leave the place a pigsty.

The following night Tina moved her books and clothes and stereo—and her vibrator—into my father's vacant room. I sat on her bed and watched her unpack. She had a prodigious wardrobe, most of it "borrowed" from local shopkeepers. I'd been with her once when she stuffed an entire pantsuit into the inner pockets of her army surplus oversized trench coat. Her motto was, "Fuck 'em if they can't take a joke."

Now and then she paused and held out a blouse or skirt for my inspection.

"Try this on," she said. "It'll look perfect on you."

To please her, I tried on a few things: a long, clingy skirt made of some satiny fabric, a see-through blouse with daisies embroidered in strategic places. These were not the kinds of clothes I was accustomed to wearing. Tina studied me, then announced that something was missing.

Reaching into a battered overnight case, she pulled out a curly blonde wig, and fit it snugly over my own dark hair. I went to the bathroom mirror to look at myself.

"I'm too pale to be blonde," I told her. "I don't have the colour."

"We can fix that," she said. "Sit down."

Obediently, I perched on the end of the bed while Tina pawed through the contents of her makeup case.

"Ruby Rouge," she said, holding a lipstick up to the light. "No, that's too dark. You need something more subtle. But bright. When's the last time you plucked your eyebrows? Green mascara, to go with your eyes. Shit, I can't find my eyelash curler."

Eventually, Tina found everything she needed and lay them all out on the bedspread beside me.

"I'm going to make you beautiful," she told me. "Now hold still and don't talk—I need to concentrate."

I've always hated being "fussed over," but it was surprisingly pleasurable, sitting there and letting her work on me. Her fingers moved with skill, painting colour on my eyelids, my cheeks, my lips, creating shadows and hollows with the expertise of a professional makeup artist. We were silent while she worked, and when she was finished she led me back to the bathroom once again.

"Not bad," I said.

"Are you kidding? You're gorgeous. You're ravishingly beautiful."

Which was an exaggeration, of course, but I was pretty damn cute, with all that paint on my face.

"You see what you're missing?" she said, as we headed back to the bedroom. "If you weren't so determined to be Miss Women's Lib, you could look like this all of the time."

"I don't think I'd have the energy," I told her. "It's too much work."

When Tina finished unpacking, we lay on her bed listening to music and drinking Pernod mixed with water from the bathroom tap. She told me she'd seen Michael; he was living in a boarding house on Cumberland Street, tree planting for the summer.

"He told me you'd broken up," she said. "It made me sad to hear it. I always thought you were such a cute couple—both of you with your long brown hair and big green eyes. You were like twins. You should get back together with that boy."

Tina always called men "boys," not all that surprising because the ones she was interested in generally were. Boys, that is. Tina lost interest in men once they turned thirty. She liked smooth, soft cheeks, chests without any hair, and slim waists. Most of all, slim waists. I often thought the boys she liked were more like girls.

"Michael hates me," I told her, surprising myself with my candour. "I necked with Pete Canary and he never got over it. We stopped having sex months ago."

"Sex is overrated," she said. "You can have sex with just about anybody. It's more important to be with someone you love. And I know Michael loved you."

"He never said so."

Tina shrugged that off. "Oh, that's Michael. He never uses the word. He's terrified of not hearing it back. But I could tell the way he looked at you that he loved you. Even if he never said it."

"Maybe. But I can't imagine being with someone who doesn't want to have sex. What kind of relationship would that be?"

"Boys are for jewelry and romance," Tina said. "For every-thing else, there's Oscar."

I was inclined to disagree, but I was getting drunk from the Pernod. When I'm drunk I go either way—I get stroppy and want to argue with everybody, or I just get very happy and believe that everybody's entitled to their own thoughts and isn't it great that we're all friends and we love each other? That was how I was feeling that night, and so I nodded and agreed with Tina. The more I thought about it, the more I realized that Michael had always been the only man for me and how could I have let him get away? It had all been a mistake; we never should have split up. Tina and I tiptoed up the stairs to the living room and she held my drink while I dialed Michael's number. After about thirteen rings, a woman answered and I hung up and went to bed.

10

Day two without power has me pacing throughout the house, like the mangy brown bears I remember from my childhood, marking out their circumscribed days in concrete pits at the zoo. The dog follows me from room to room, unaccustomed to all this activity. I should sit down and write, but I can't settle. When will this bloody storm die down?

How quiet it is without electricity! This must be what the pioneers experienced, days of silence, nothing much to look at as the snow continued to fall. It's a kind of sensory deprivation that encourages deep introspection. Or boredom. They must have been desperately bored at times, especially the women. Women, in my experience, tend to have more imagination than men. They can only too easily imagine themselves living another kind of life, one not limited by the boundaries of rock and water and trees. They can't always have been thrilled with hours of housework and needlepoint, child-rearing and baking. There must have been times when they wanted to throw themselves off the nearest high precipice, if only the snow would stop long enough for them to get out.

"God save me from the farm," my grandmother wrote in her diary. She worked five and a half days a week in the bank, cleaned house, went to church and taught Sunday School, studied German, shorthand, and Latin, and was no stranger to hard work. But she never wanted to go back to living in the country. It was the boredom, the isolation, that she feared. Civilized people need contact, even if it's only the mailman, or the guy from hydro coming to read your meter.

Grandma's diary is one of the few books I brought with me

on this trip. I like to read sections from it when the writing's slow, or when, like today, I have time on my hands and am feeling nostalgiac. She began it on her eighteenth birthday, and on that day she wrote, "Sometimes when I think of passing the rest of my life in this place, always doing the same thing, I feel as if I would like to catch the first train and go anywhere."

She was a stenographer at the bank—a pretty good one, she admits: "When I was away down to Ohio this summer, they found it hard to get along without me."

But her job didn't satisfy her. She wanted to finish her schooling, which had been cut short at sixteen; she dreamed of someday going to college.

The opportunity arose a few years later when a gentleman friend offered to borrow the money to allow her to go to university. Her fiancé—my grandfather—objected to the idea and in the end she talked herself out of it. On 19 August 1915, she wrote:

> *I will keep up my languages as well as I can; read lots of the best books and try to improve my mind as much as possible . . . I would like to make a success of married life if I ever tried it and I have sense enough to know that a knowledge of French and German will not help me to—well, make pies, for instance.*

Fifty years later, when I told her I was thinking about not going on to university, she wouldn't hear of it. She was determined that I, who am like her in so many ways, should not turn down any of life's opportunities. Grandma made great pies, and she read everything under the sun. She went on to become a teller at the Royal Bank, one of the first women to do so, and was transferred across the country to work in Calgary. But she never got to write BA after her name. I believe she always regretted it.

Margie Taylor

Curled up in the wicker armchair by the window, I spend the afternoon rereading the entries in this book. No mention of the sinking of the Titanic, but the Halifax explosion is recorded, and the Winnipeg general strike. And, of course, the First World War, in which her brother—my great-uncle—died at Vimy Ridge.

"This is the first break in our family circle," she writes, "the first real trouble we have ever known. May God help us to bear it as we should."

They receive the usual letters saying he was killed instantly and didn't suffer; you wonder how many of those letters were written, and how many of them were true. Another brother survives the war but is permanently, psychically damaged.

When Grandma was alive, we always went down to city hall on Remembrance Day for the laying of the wreaths. All those years of turning up for the ceremony at the Cenotaph, grey heads remembering the lost young men, old soldiers wrapped in their long coats as the first flakes of winter began to drift down from the slate-grey skies. My grandmother in her good black fur, her paper poppy brilliant against the glistening pelts. The granite soldier in the old-fashioned uniform, leaning on his gun. I thought he was beautiful and vaguely disappointed. We had let him down, it seemed to me, we had let down all those beautiful young men, sent them off to die in foreign places and forgotten about them. Except for one day each year when we stood in silence, shivered in the cold, and made ourselves think about unknown relatives, dead long before we were born and buried "somewhere in France."

> *They shall grow not old, as we that are left grow old;*
> *Age shall not weary them, nor the years condemn.*
> *At the going down of the sun and in the morning*
> *We will remember them.*

✄ ✄ ✄

By 4 PM the storm appears to be letting up; the snow is still falling, lightly, but the wind has died down and the sun is struggling to break through. The dog rouses himself from his place by the stove and pads over to the door, letting me know he needs to go out.

"All right, boy, let me just finish this last page."

It's my favourite part, this section—Friday, 30 October, 1920:

"I have been a mother for two weeks," my grandmother writes. "Our baby girl was born on Friday, 15 October, at 8:10 PM."

My mother, eight pounds, six ounces—a "big fat baby girl." In those days they used chloroform so you gave birth during what they called "twilight sleep," and they kept you in hospital for ten days. Now you're more likely to get a couple of hours before they chuck you out. And few women of my generation have their mothers and maiden aunts on hand to help take care of the newborn.

Still, they got rid of the chloroform; some things have definitely improved.

11

THE POWER COMES ON AGAIN THE FOLLOWING
morning. I call Liz, reconnecting myself with the outside world.
She sounds relieved to hear me.

"I was worried about you," she says. "Are you okay?"

"I'm fine, but I think I'm snowed in. What's it like in
town?"

"Ridiculous. Nobody's going anywhere. The guy on the
radio says we've had as much snow so far this year as we usually get all winter, can you believe it? At least it gave me a chance
to clean out the upstairs closet. I've been meaning to get to that
for ages. How about you?"

Not wanting to confess that I went out and got lost in the
storm, I tell her I read my grandmother's diary and did some
writing. It sounds a little unproductive, so I add that I also
hemmed a pair of pants. Which is a lie. I hate that Liz brings
out this ridiculous need in me to compete for the title of domes-
tic goddess. Who really cares if I have ten-year-old dust bunnies
lurking under the couch? It didn't used to matter: we used to
brag, she and I, that we hadn't done housework since our kids
were born, wouldn't know where to find the iron on a bet. I
miss the old Liz; sometimes I wonder if we'd even be friends if
we met now, rather than thirty years ago.

"Anyway," she says, "I'm glad you called. What are you
doing Saturday night?"

A loaded question. "Why?"

"Joan's having a 'fuckerware' party. Kind of like a
Tupperware party but with edible panties. Want to come?"

"Sorry, Liz. I don't think so."

"It's for a good cause. The money's all going to charity."

"Why not just write out a cheque?"

"Because," she says, as if I'm a small and rather stupid child, "parties are more fun. Remember fun, Alex? A bunch of people getting together to socialize and have a good time? I think you've been out at the lake too long. You need to get out more."

I defend myself by telling her I have lunch every Tuesday with Joan, but she dismisses that.

"That's not socializing," she says. "That's sitting around talking about dead people and it sounds rather morbid, if you want my opinion. I'll probably go, anyway. It's fine for you—you're married. We single women have to keep up with these things."

The phone rings again and it's Joan inviting me to the party. Again, I beg off.

"But I'd be happy to make a donation," I tell her. "What's the charity?"

"It's not a charity, exactly. I'm involved with a breast cancer support group—we meet once a month. One of the younger women is a single parent with two small kids. The money's for her."

I haven't thought about Joan having a life apart from our weekly lunches. And now it turns out she's involved with a cancer support group—what else don't I know?

Reading my mind, Joan suggests we do something different next Tuesday—have lunch at her place.

"I want you to see the house," she says, "and I have something for you."

"For me? What is it?"

"Just something you should probably have," she says. "If you change your mind about the party, call me."

Margie Taylor

She and I have just hung up when Boo Montgomery arrives to plow me out. I watch from the window as, in less than five minutes, he clears a wide swath through the snowdrifts outside my door. As he makes his final retreat back up to the main road, I step outside and call to him: "Boo! Thanks! What do I owe you?"

He leans his head out of his open window, indicates that he can't hear me, the engine is too loud. So I hurry over to where he's brought the snowplow to a temporary halt and repeat the question: "You did a great job—what do I owe you?"

A huge, bearded man with what would be a magnificent smile were he not missing his upper front teeth, Boo grins and shakes his head.

"Don't worry about it," he says. "We'll see how many times you need me and settle up at Christmas."

The missing teeth cause him to lisp in a manner that I find charming, in a perverse sort of way. I thank him again and he drives off, spitting up snow and diesel fumes in his wake.

The sound of the tractor fades in the distance. I stand for a moment out on the driveway, enjoying the warmth of the sun after two days trapped inside. The temperature's rising. I can feel my spirits lifting with each clump of snow that drops suddenly from the trees with a muffled *thunk*.

✖ ✖ ✖

When giving me the directions to her house, Joan said it was easy to find—just off Vickers Park. After all these years, the name still conjures up images of money: gracious old houses sheltered by maples, birch, and trembling aspen, home to a clutch of doctors, and dentists, and one particularly successful madam. Nowadays the doctors and dentists have moved out to

the suburbs. But the houses, even the ones that are a little ramshackle and untended, retain their aura of gentility. Red brick
and sandstone, with solid front porches that people still use,
I'm willing to bet. Driving through the once-familiar streets,
I'm possessed by the familiar feeling of being an outsider and
wishing the course of circumstance had allowed me to end up
here, in this neighbourhood, living one of these lives.

I pull up in front of a three-storey dwelling whose front
yard looks tidy and cared-for. The path leading up to the porch
has been neatly shovelled and the bushes are covered in sack-
ing. Joan greets me at the front door, cradling a large white and
grey tomcat in her arms.

"This is Maximillian," she tells me, giving him a hug, a gesture he doesn't appear to appreciate. He struggles to get free
and she sets him down on the floor, watching him with obvious
affection.

"Max is the boss of the place, he pushes the rest of us
around. Don't you, Max, you bad old pussycat?"

Her mother hates him, Joan says: he jumps on to her lap
whenever she's there and scares the hell out of her. "She's
never liked cats, which is one reason I love them."

I hand her the bottle of wine I brought and bend down to
take off my boots.

"Does your mother live near here?"

"Good Lord, no," she says, looking at me as if I'd suggested
something particularly gruesome. "She lives in Florida, but she
visits twice a year. Max gets banished to the backyard, and I
wind up with a migraine. It takes us a week to recuperate after
she's gone. Come on, I'll give you the tour."

The dark hardwood floors smell of polish and a magnificent
bouquet of hothouse gladioli adorn a table in the hallway. Joan
tells me the house belonged to her grandfather; her mother was

born here. At the back is a long, narrow garden, which she says is overgrown in the summer with wildflowers—what her mother would call weeds. Joan says she likes things to be left in their "natural" state.

"Mom insists I keep up appearances in the front, but I'm allowed to do what I want with the back. Which means I do nothing."

After telling me to sit down and make myself comfortable, Joan takes a bottle of liqueur from a cupboard and puts a kettle on the stove.

"We'll start with tea and Grand Marnier," she says. "We'll have the wine with lunch."

Waiting for the kettle to boil, I have a chance to admire the kitchen. It's immaculate without feeling sterile, the kind of room you want to spend a lot of time in, drinking tea and coffee and talking with friends. Joan tells me the "fuckerware" party went well—they raised five hundred dollars—more, with my donation.

"I had the living room decked out like Martha Stewart," Joan says, "and nobody left the kitchen."

"It's a great room," I tell her. "It's a terrific house—you must have missed it when you were in Montreal. Are you happy to be back?"

"Are you?"

"I asked you first."

Joan gets up to make the tea and says nothing until she's added the Grand Marnier, pouring the hot amber liquid into our glasses. She hands me mine, raises hers in a toast: "To friendship," she says.

"To friendship."

"Most of the time," she says, settling back into her chair, "yes, I'm glad I'm back. It's been five years now. I've gotten used to the winters and the smell of the mill. I know the good restaurants and the ones to avoid. I miss the anonymity of a big city, but I like having friends close by. I guess it's a mix, if you know what I mean."

"Life is a trade-off," I tell her. "My sister used to say that."

She nods as if I've said something truly profound, and says, "What about you? What's it like for you being back?"

"It's a little different for me, staying out at the lake. It's not like being in town."

She tells me that's not really an answer, so I try a little harder.

"How I feel being back here is how I felt when I grew up here—like a fish out of water. But that's how I feel just about everywhere, so I'm used to it. It'd be nice to fit in somewhere, but maybe some people never get that. I don't know."

"You must feel you belong in Vancouver," she says. "I mean, you've been living there for years, right?"

"I felt it when the kids were young. Motherhood gives you a place in the world—it's like wearing a name tag: 'Hi, I'm a Mom.' When the kids left I had to come up with a new tag, and I haven't figured it out yet. And then David left—"

Too late, I realize I've given away more than I intended. Joan is looking at me in that certain way. I'm afraid if we continue I'll get maudlin and I hate people who do that.

"So—what's this mysterious thing you want to give me? I'm dying of curiosity."

Joan stands up, tells me to take my tea and follow her. We make our way up two sets of stairs to a small room at the top of the house, overlooking the street. This must have been a bedroom, once, or perhaps the maid's room; Joan's turned it into a kind of sitting room-cum-office, all chintz and billowy curtains and arrangements of dried flowers. There are two large, overstuffed armchairs and she directs me into one of them, while she sets her glass down on the floor and drags a box from the closet.

"It's in here somewhere," she says. "I found it after the funeral."

She's talking about Tina. She went out there the day after the funeral, out to the lake where she died.

"I'd given her a sweater," she says, taking books and photo albums out of the box and setting them on the floor beside her. "My mother bought it for me and it was kind of a fuchsia colour. Mother knows I can't wear fuchsia, which is probably why she bought it. Anyway, I thought Tina might like it so I gave it to her. And she did, she wore it a lot. When she died, I figured I'd go out to the cabin and see if I could find the sweater. You know—to remember her by."

She continues to rummage through the box while I sip my tea and gaze around the room. "Shit, I know it's here somewhere. I've been carrying it around with me for years."

"I don't know if I'd wear a fuchsia sweater myself, Joan—"

"No, no, not the sweater—oh, good, here it is. I knew I still had it."

From the depths of the cardboard box Joan brings out a small object, wrapped in several layers of tissue paper, and hands it to me. It's a brown leather diary, a small one, the kind you get when you're a teenager, with room for five years of notes.

"Tina's?" I ask.

She nods. "It was in the top drawer of her dresser. Under the sweater, funnily enough. I don't know why I took it; maybe I thought there'd be something in it, some clue about what happened to her. There isn't," she adds, getting up from the floor and settling into the other armchair. "It was all written years before she met Conrad. And she'd cut out some pages that might have had something incriminating on them, something she didn't want people to see. At least, I assumed she was the one who cut out the pages. I can't think who else would have done it. Anyway, I want you to have it."

I turn the little book over in my hands and trace the faded gilt lettering on the cover: FIVE YEAR DIARY, on a background of tiny fleur-de-lis. It feels very familiar; I had one almost exactly like this when I was twelve. Inside the front cover she's written her name: Erika Kristina Van Buren.

"I was surprised to find it," Joan says. "I thought everything went up in flames."

When Conrad died, Tina wanted to cremate his body out at the lake, build a pyre of leaves and tree branches and have the blood of an animal—preferably a wolf—poured on to the flames. This was how the Greeks and Romans cremated their warriors: a hero's burial.

"It was Marianne's idea," Joan says. "Tina's sister. She had some weird kind of hold over Tina. People used to say she was a witch. Of course, his family told them to forget it, they weren't about to have anything to do with funeral pyres or anything like that. So Marianne decided they should build a fire on the beach and burn everything that had any attachment to him. She said it was the only way to purify Conrad's soul; it had to go up in smoke."

And so they made a fire of driftwood and dead branches and burned Tina's letters from Conrad, the photographs she had of the two of them—even the last copy of the magazine, the one with her picture on the cover.

I can't believe Tina would allow that to burn, but Joan swears it's true. Tina described it for her: Marianne tearing out the pages, one by one, and putting them into the fire, saving the cover for last. At the very last minute Tina wanted to stop her,

she didn't want to see her face—all pink lipstick and pigtails—
go up in smoke. But Marianne insisted. She tore the picture in
half and fed the pieces into the fire.

Afterwards, Marianne lifted her hands towards the heavens
like a high priestess.

"It is done," she said.

And it was.

Except that this small, childish diary, dating back ten years
before Tina's death, survived.

"Are you sure you don't want to keep it?" I ask.

But Joan is adamant. I get the sense she's relieved, in a way,
to have found someone to give it to. "I've always felt a little
weird about hanging on to it," she says. "It wasn't mine to take
in the first place."

✳ ✳ ✳

By the time I'm ready to leave, it's almost five o-clock. Joan
accompanies me to the porch while I get my boots on, and hands
me my coat. The eastern sky is beginning to darken into a surreal
shade of blue that is closer to violet, while in the west the sun is
spreading a brilliant scarlet radiance all along the horizon.

"Top *that*, Hollywood," she says.

"It is beautiful, isn't it? My father always used to say we had
the best sunsets in this part of the world. Something to do with
the dust, I think."

"Is he still alive, your dad?"

I shake my head. "No, he died years ago. Before the kids
were born. How about yours?"

"He's in St. Ignatius. On the fourth floor."

St. Ignatius is the old convent turned nursing home up on
the hill, overlooking the harbour. The fourth floor, I know, is

reserved for Alzheimer's patients. Joan says her father was diagnosed with the disease six years ago—it's one of the reasons she decided to move back.

"Mother couldn't cope—well, she claimed she couldn't, anyway. And maybe she was telling the truth. Anyway, the decision was made to put him into care, and she wanted me to come back and help with the details. And then, once we got him in there, she divorced him and moved to the States."

The shock must show in my face.

"It does sound pretty callous, doesn't it?" she says. "To be fair, Dad doesn't know anything about it. He's in his own world, doesn't recognize me and didn't recognize Mother, either, when she was still going to see him. He has no idea she's left him and if he did know, I don't think he'd care. I go three or four times a week, and he's very cheerful, always in a good mood. Much happier now than I remember him being when I was growing up. He calls me Isobel. It's the name of a girl he went out with years ago, before he met Mother."

"Does he ever ask about your mom?"

Joan shakes her head. "Never. He never asks about anyone. It's the nature of the disease, I guess. I'm just glad that for him, anyway, it seems to be a pleasant experience. Wherever he's gone to, in his mind, he seems to be happy enough to be there."

She gives me a quick hug. "It's great having you to talk to, you know that? You don't judge—I feel I can tell you anything."

"I'm in no position to judge anyone, believe me," I tell her. And it's true, but I know what she means. All most of us really want is a receptive, uncritical ear. Doesn't sound like much to ask, but you almost never find it.

12

IF SKETCHING OUT THE DETAILS OF A LIFE LIVED IS like mining for gold, then diaries are the motherlode. Think of the journals that Katherine Mansfield and Virginia Woolf left behind, or Henry Crabb Robinson, who counted Goethe, Worsdworth, and Coleridge among his friends. What would we have lost if Samuel Pepys had decided to burn his diaries, or if Boswell had not thought Dr. Johnson worth writing about?

Tina, unfortunately, was not that kind of diarist. Unlike my grandmother, whose journals contained detailed information about her work, her family, and her dreams, the sad, cryptic entries in this little book reveal very little about Tina. The very first entry, dated Tuesday, 14 June 1966, is not even written by her:

> *I love you more than anything else in the world.*
> *You may have lots to remember that you won't forgive*
> *me for, but think of what I've got to remember.*
> *You are a first-class bitch that has eaten away a major*
> *portion of my heart (rotten).*
> *I love you so much that it is obvious to everyone but you.*
> *Click your fingers & I'll always be yours.*
> *Yours forever*
> *Lawrence*

Who the hell is Lawrence, I wonder? No idea. The next entries after that are dated October 1967:

> *Wed Oct. 11: Saw Michael after work.*
> *Thurs Oct. 12: Supposed to meet M. for lunch but didn't*
>   *make it. Slept in.*

There's a long gap, and then we're into 1968:

*Thurs Feb. 22: Went to hockey game. Got letter and
$100 from Mother. Michael & I finished.
Fri Feb. 23: Phoned Lawrence. Slept most of day. Went
to see M. at garage—wouldn't speak to me.*

By this time, Tina was working at the Ontario Hospital,
later known as the Lakehead Psychiatric Hospital. She told me
once that this was the job that got her hooked on amphetamines. Eventually, she was caught stealing drugs and was fired,
but the diary says nothing about that. What she records is the
minutiae of life: getting a cheque from the hospital, hating her
job, having her phone disconnected. She continues to see
Lawrence while going out with Michael—*Phoned Lawrence in
morning. Fought with M. at night. Went home.*

And that is pretty much the pattern. There is the odd cryptic entry like this one:

*Thurs March 7: Went to court re Lawrence—remanded
till 28th. Saw M.'s sister.
Sat March 16: Left O.H. today—under rather undesir-
able conditions.*

In the fall of 1968, she starts taking classes at Lakehead
University, majoring in English. Her mother and sister come
up from Toronto to visit, and Tina says she can't get over how
beautiful Marianne is.

*Fri Nov. 15: Michael and I took them for supper at Uncle
Frank's. Mother was positively embarrassing—
kept telling Michael cute little anecdotes about
when I was a mere child.*

The next day she and her sister aren't talking, and by the
time they leave for Toronto, Tina's relieved. The following
month, she writes that her mother and father are getting a
divorce and her sister still isn't speaking to her. The next few
entries after that sound sad, even though she's met a new man:

*Fri Dec. 13: In love again—this time more painful than
    any other.*
*Sun Dec. 15: Very depressed. Studied for English exam.
    Went to see D. who never came.*
*Mon Dec. 16: English exam, 9 to 11. Science exam, 2:30
    to 5:30. Depressed.*
*Tues Dec. 17: History exam, 9 to 12. Seemed to be best of
    all exams. Mom and Marianne left for Europe
    today. Sure wish I was going as well—no bread &
    Mother's broke after paying off my retarded father.*
*Fri Dec. 20: D. left to go skiing. Depressed. Lawrence
    came over.*
*Sat Dec. 21: Everyone off to bus, airport, etc. Depressed.
    Lawrence left his car for me. Went to sleep early.*
*Severe storm. 10:10: Listening to radio, feeling no pain
    at moment.*
And the last entry in the little brown book:
*Tue Dec. 31: New Year's Eve dance in the Great Hall.
    Went with Michael, left with Lawrence. Happy
    1969.*

Not much to go on. Of course, she wasn't writing it for
me—she wasn't keeping a record for posterity. Interesting that
it ends just a couple of weeks before her "big break," as she
used to call it, with a laugh: her modelling session for Maclean's
magazine.

I didn't know her then, but she told me about it, in detail,
several times. She had assumed that the magazine cover
would lead to a real modelling career, not just the scattering of
small-town fashion jobs that made up her resumé so far. When
that didn't happen, she put it down to her weight—she wasn't
skinny enough to make it in the big leagues.

She once told me that when the magazine came out, she
called the publisher and ordered two hundred copies. Every
time she went to bed with a new man, she said, she gave him a
copy of that magazine, with her picture on the cover. By the

time I met her, she had only one left—she kept it locked in a chest under the bed.

I believed the story, and I repeated it—well, who wouldn't? It was such a Tina kind of story. Now, though, it occurs to me that it was probably just that—a story. Like her mother's wrinkle. Even Tina Van Buren was unlikely to have slept with 199 men in a two-year period—although she may have come close.

13

THE DOG IS SICK. HE HASN'T BEEN WELL FOR THE past couple of days but I've written it off to old age and the weather. It's cold and he doesn't want to be out as long. Our walks are truncated, we get to the top of the road, where the railway tracks begin, and he wants to turn around.

We haven't made it all the way to Tina's old cabin since the snowstorm, and in a way, I'm glad. If I was obsessed with Tina before I arrived, those daily pilgrimages to the cabin were making it worse. I'd be better off in the library, going through the microfiche, or having lunch with Joan Dawson.

Which is what I'm planning to do today, after I take the dog to the vet. Last night he vomited up his dinner and this morning he wouldn't eat. I called the animal clinic in town and they said to bring him in, which turns out to be harder than it sounds. He knows something is up, and refuses to get into the car. I offer him a chance to sit up front, beside me, normally a surefire technique, but he backs away from the car with mournful, sidelong looks as if he knows what I'm up to and cannot believe I'd try to pull this old trick on him.

"Look," I say, "we're just going for a ride. Don't you want to go for a ride? I'll give you a biscuit." (Another usually guaranteed approach; he discovered the word "biscuit" when we were living in England and has always associated it with the most sublime treats. "Cookie" leaves him cold.)

I'm standing out here freezing, trying to reason with an extremely stubborn old dog. Eventually I take him by the collar and alternately drag, push, and lift him into the back seat where he immediately flops down, resigned to his fate. I hold out the biscuit, feeling that I need to live up to my promises. He stares sadly at it for a moment, as if debating whether it would be better to take the biscuit and eat it, or refuse it and punish me. In the end, he takes it from my hand and swallows it in two noisy gulps.

"You can't be all that sick. You've still got an appetite."

This, of course, doesn't merit a response. His treat gone, he turns his head away from me, lays it down on his two front paws, and stares at the back of the front car seat, depression personified.

✖ ✖ ✖

If it was difficult getting the dog into the car, getting him out once we've reached the clinic is practically impossible. His intuition, which he shares with women and all intelligent mammals, tells him there is danger here. He backs into the far corner of the seat and holds himself rigid, refusing to be budged. The offer of yet another biscuit, held just beyond his reach, fails to move him. I walk around the back of the car to the other door, and he moves away just as I get there. We could do this all morning; it's ridiculous. Just as I'm beginning to feel desperate, a lean, attractive man in a leather bomber jacket and earmuffs comes up to the car, and asks if he can give me a hand.

"It's my dog," I tell him, wondering if I remembered to brush my hair before I left this morning. Living alone makes you forget about your appearance. "I can't get him out of the car."

The man peers into the back seat and smiles. He has a truly wonderful smile. "A Black Lab. Great dog," he says.

"Great but stubborn," I tell him. We're standing so close to each other I can smell his cologne—or aftershave. Do men still wear aftershave? I love a man who smells good.

90

Margie Taylor

"It's all right, old fella." The man crouches down outside the open car door and holds out a hand. "Come on, buddy, I'm not going to hurt you. Come say hello."

To my amazement, the dog pulls himself up off his haunches and sidles towards the stranger, resting his muzzle in the man's outstretched palm and allowing himself to be rubbed behind the ears.

"He loves that," I say, and the stranger nods.

"They all do. Especially Labs." He studies the dog and gently pulls at the upper eyelids, one by one. "He hasn't been feeling very well, has he?"

"No, he's not himself. He threw up last night."

"Diarrhea?"

"I don't know. I'm not sure. Not in the house, but maybe outside. Do you know about dogs?"

"A little. It's what they pay me for." He straightens up, and turns to me, holding out his hand. "Jim Bennet." He indicates the clinic and adds, "I work here."

"Oh, you're the vet." He has a nice, firm handshake. And very blue eyes. "I'm Alex Cooper and this is Jake. You're who we're coming to see."

Jim the vet smiles and turns back to the dog. "Come on, Jake. Let's go see what we can do for you."

And without a minute's hesitation, the dog steps from the back seat on to the sidewalk and stands there looking up at his newfound friend with his tongue hanging out, the picture of compliance. The vet goes over to the door and holds it open for us. I bend down to fasten the dog's leash on to his collar.

"Thanks a bunch," I whisper, as I struggle with the metal clasp. "Won't get out of the car for me and you'll follow this guy anywhere. Traitor."

The dog gives me an excuse-me-do-I-know-you kind of look

before trotting happily over to Dr. Jim. He thrusts himself against the doctor's legs, the suckhole, and receives an affectionate pat in return. I wonder if he, too, likes the way the doctor smells.

✳ ✳ ✳

In the examining room, the dog sits quietly on a metal examining table and lets Dr. Jim gently poke and prod him, peer into his mouth and take his temperature. While he does this, the doctor asks me about myself—where am I from, what family I have. I tell him I'm from here, originally, meaning Thunder Bay, and he looks surprised.

"Really?"

Just as I'm wondering how I should take that, he adds, "I'm new to the Lakehead and so far, every single person I've met is from someplace else. You're my first homegrown patient."

"I've been living in Vancouver for more than twenty years. My children were born there."

"Beautiful city," he says. "Somehow, though, when I'm out there, everybody just seems a little smug, if you know what I mean."

I know what he means: two million people spending their lives sopping wet under cloudy skies, congratulating themselves for living on the correct side of the Rockies.

He wants to know what brought me home and I tell him I'm writing a novel, surprising myself that I've just come out and said it. Perhaps I'm trying to impress him, wanting to let him know I'm not your average middle-aged dog owner.

"A novel. Hey, that's terrific. Good for you. I tried to write a novel once but I couldn't get past the first paragraph. So I became a vet instead."

It occurs to me there's lots of people out there writing novels who would've been better off becoming veterinarians, and I tell him so.

He grins. "Right. Stick to what you're good at."

❊ ❊ ❊

The verdict isn't hopeful: a cyst that may or may not be cancer. The age of the dog is against him and although his teeth are in good shape and he still loves to chase a stick—or a squirrel— there's no getting around the fact that in human terms he's close to a hundred.

"I'd like to do some blood tests and a couple of x-rays," the vet tells me, his hand stroking the dog's handsome, broad head. "Why don't you leave him here overnight and come back tomorrow? I should have a better idea by then."

"Overnight?"

I don't like the idea of walking out and leaving him there. We never leave him anymore. When he was younger we occasionally took him to the kennel if we were going to be out of town for a few days. He would be hysterical with relief and hoarse from barking when we got back. Eventually one of us would stay behind, or we'd pay somebody to come in and house-sit.

"He'll be fine. Won't you, boy?" Dr. Jim takes the dog's head in his hands and gives him a quick, rough caress. The dog licks his hand, devotion shining in his dark brown eyes. The vet laughs.

"We're pals, aren't we, fella?" To me, he adds, "I'll take him back to the house tonight. He'll hang out with my dogs and have the run of the place. He'll hardly know you're gone."

"Can you do that? Take him back to your place, I mean?"

"I live in the country," he says, "out on Dawson Road. There's lots of room for him to run around—kind of a doggie country club."

I don't like the idea of leaving him, but it's obvious the dog's happy to stay with the vet, and I don't blame him: if I were twenty years younger and single, I'd be angling to stay myself. So I leave my dog at the clinic—a young woman with purple hair and a silver ring pierced through her eyebrow takes his leash and walks us to the door.

"He'll be fine," she says, "don't you worry. Dr. Jim's awesome with dogs—he, like, has a way with them, eh? Labs especially. He's crazy about Labs." She asks me if there's anything in particular they should know about the dog, any likes or dislikes, and I can't really think of anything—he's just your typical, all-round friendly Black Lab. And then I remember one thing:

"Belts," I tell her, and the young woman gives me a quizzical look. "He's got this thing about belts. Men's belts, in particular. And belt buckles. We're not sure, we think he might have been hit with a belt when he was a pup. But any time my husband forgets and goes to take off his belt around him, the dog just goes crazy. He gets really upset—it's the only time he's ever looked ready to attack."

"Really?" The girl looks at the dog with renewed curiosity. "Isn't that interesting? So you don't like belts, eh, boy? Well, don't you worry, nobody's going to hurt you here."

"You will tell the doctor that, will you?" I ask. "I'd hate to have him get lunged at or something—"

"Don't you worry," she says, stooping down to give the dog a quick hug. "You're gonna love it here, aren't you, boy? Isn't that right? Aren't you gonna just love it?"

And the dog, who has obviously forgotten all about me, rewards her with a lavish display of tongue-licking, moaning in delight. I leave them to their bonding, and back out of the driveway feeling slightly irritated. It's one thing for the dog to adapt to new surroundings; it's another, I think, for him to let fourteen years of devoted care and attention go right down the toilet.

✕ ✕ ✕

The trip to the vet has left me depressed; Joan insists on ordering dessert for a change, to cheer me up, and we decide on one of the house coffees: the Canuck's Special, which contains rum and maple syrup. When it comes, it's not bad—a little on the sweet side and topped with enough whipped cream to sink a ship.

"Normally," Joan tells me, dipping her dessert spoon into the mountain of cream, "I'd be riddled with guilt, ordering something like this. But I've decided to allow myself one day a week to indulge myself. Every Tuesday I'm going to look the other way if I eat too much or drink too much or forget to think good thoughts."

"Do you really do that? Make a point of thinking good thoughts?"

She nods and takes another spoonful of cream. "Absolutely. I have to. It's part of the new me I created when I got cancer. Think three good thoughts each day, preferably about someone you don't like. My mother is my biggest challenge—I've really had to dig deep to come up with three good thoughts about her."

"So what did you come up with?"

She sighs, puts down her spoon, and counts them out on her fingers: "She doesn't drink, she's good at playing bridge, and she taught me to sit up straight."

"That's it?"

Joan picks up her spoon and resumes eating. "Pretty much. Now and then I manage to come up with something new but those three are the basics. So when will you know? About the dog, I mean."

"Dr. Jim says he'll do some blood tests, and they'll take about a week. But he can give me a pretty good idea tomorrow, after the x-ray."

"Do you know you've mentioned Dr. Jim three times in the past hour?" Joan says. "Can I infer anything from that?"

"You can infer anything you like," I say, pushing my coffee to one side. "But you'd be wrong. This stuff is way too sweet—I'm going to order a decaf."

"But he's cute, right?" Joan persists.

"Yes, he's cute. He's also fifteen years younger than me."

"That shouldn't stop you. Younger men can be great, if you pick the right one."

"I had my younger man fling, Joan. And it was a mistake."

Joan continues eating, very deliberately. After a moment she says, "Do you want to talk about it? I'll understand if you'd rather not."

"It's not that. It's just—look, I'd really appreciate it if you didn't tell Liz about this. Do you mind?"

"Why on earth would I tell Liz? Or anybody?"

"Liz has always thought David was the ideal man for me. She thinks we have the perfect marriage. It's the only thing she's ever envied about me. I guess I'd like to keep it that way."

"My lips are sealed," Joan promises.

It's a relief, in a way, to finally talk about it. Almost a year since the affair ended, and till now I haven't spoken about it with anyone—not David, not any of my friends in Vancouver. They, like Liz, think David's the perfect man—the perfect husband. I used to think so too.

Margie Taylor

Sometimes I wonder when it started to change—when did I begin to resent his opinions, when did I start leaving the room at parties every time some young woman began to hover around, gazing up at him with a flirtatious reverence and seeking his advice? Most likely about the same time I realized that although I was so much younger than David, and he was still playing the teacher, I was no longer his student. I was sick of the performance on both our parts.

As I tell Joan, my real regret is that I wasn't brave enough to be honest with him.

"I think if I'd just told him how I felt, we could have dealt with it. David's not an unreasonable person, he's willing to accept that things don't always go the way you want them to. I should have told him."

"So why didn't you?"

"I didn't want to let him down. I didn't want to disappoint him."

"So you took solace elsewhere."

"Yes. I took solace elsewhere. I went to bed with one of his grad students. He was almost twenty years younger than me. Talk about Freud—it was a veritable case study."

"Did David find out?"

"No, I don't think so."

I couldn't believe I could ever really keep anything from David. He knew me so well—surely he suspected something all those nights when I was suddenly busy with a special project, suddenly had to be out of the house so much. He must have known. But he said nothing.

The affair ended. David and I carried on, but I pretended to be asleep when he came to bed. You'd think I'd have been relieved I'd gotten away with it. Instead, I was angry at David for not noticing.

"Anyway, things between us have just gone on as usual. At least, they did before he went on sabbatical. We pretend that everything's normal, but it's not."

"Normal doesn't exist," Joan says. "Normal's about as realistic as *Leave it to Beaver*—whenever somebody doesn't like what you're doing, they accuse you of not being normal. I've never believed in normal, myself. I've never trusted it."

"Tina said something like that to me, once. A long time ago."

"I'm not surprised. Tina didn't care what anybody thought. I always liked that about her."

Joan sets aside her empty glass and nods at the waitress, who's come to drop off the bill and clear the table.

"Tell me something," she says, as we get ready to leave. "Are you thinking of telling David what happened? Because, if you want my advice—don't. Confession may be good for the soul, but it doesn't do much for a marriage."

14

PEOPLE ARE ALWAYS KIND WHEN THEY'VE GOT BAD news to deliver. Nikki, the girl with purple hair, greets me with a sad little smile and an offer of a cup of tea—herbal, with unpasteurized honey.

"Why don't you have a seat?" she says. "Dr. Jim will just be a few minutes."

In the back of the clinic, behind closed doors, a dog is letting the world know he's unhappy about being kept prisoner here. I leaf through "DOGS: the Magazine for Animal Lovers" and am halfway through a piece about the effect of too much protein in the diet (makes dogs neurotic, apparently), when a door opens and Dr. Jim walks over to me, his hand held out in welcome.

"Hi, there. Sorry to keep you waiting." He guides me back behind the counter into his office, indicates a chair, then shuts the door behind us. I've been expecting to be taken back to see Jake. This detour can't be a good sign.

"Is he all right?"

The vet plants himself on top of his desk, just inches from me, and takes one of my hands in his. The feeling of his strong, warm skin against mine unnerves me. I have to force myself to concentrate on what he's saying.

"I'm afraid the old boy isn't doing too well," he begins.

I feel my eyes suddenly, unexpectedly, fill up with tears. I'm emotional these days—the slightest thing makes me cry—and I'm afraid I'm going to break down and embarrass myself.

Dr. Jim gives my hand a compassionate squeeze, which only makes me feel worse.

"What's wrong with him?" I ask.

Pulmonary metastasis. Cancerous lesions to the lungs, both of them. The x-ray showed it immediately; there was no need for a biopsy. Too far gone for radiation or drug therapy. Even if it wasn't, he's an old dog—too old to stand such treatment.

"If he was a few years younger—we can do amazing things these days, it's really remarkable. But given his age, well, I can't in all honesty recommend it."

"Is he in pain?"

"No, not at the moment, but eventually he will be. He's uncomfortable, especially if he tries to run or move about too much, but we've got pills we can give him to take away most of the discomfort. The thing is, in a very short time he's going to be really sick. You might want to think about sparing him all that. Letting him go while he's still in pretty good shape with a good quality of life."

"You mean putting him to sleep."

He nods, gets up and walks around to the other side of his desk, slumps into his chair, and stares glumly at me.

"It never gets any easier to tell people they need to make these kinds of decisions. A dog like yours is part of the family— I hate to have to sit here and tell you there's nothing I can do for him."

I begin to tell him the money's not a problem, but he interrupts me.

"I'm sure it's not. Unfortunately, all money can do at this stage is buy us a little more time. A month or two at the most. We can't cure him. I'm sorry."

You can tell he really is sorry. I wish there was something I could say to make both of us feel better. What will I tell Kate and Adam? I'll have to phone them when I get back to the lake, tell them I've brought their dog (because he always was their dog,

Kate's in particular) halfway across the country only to have to put him down. They won't blame me, but maybe if we'd stayed in Vancouver he wouldn't be sick. It would have happened eventually, of course, but he might have had another year or two if we'd just stayed put.

Dr. Jim tells me he'll understand if I want a second opinion; he says he can give me the names of two other vets in the city whose opinion he respects, but I shake my head: "No, I trust you." Which is true; I've met this man twice and I'd trust him with my life. "When do I have to decide?"

"I'll give you a prescription for some painkillers and some pills to clear up the diarrhea. Nikki'll give you a special diet plan, a little extra nutrition and fibre. You can take him home today and call me back when you've decided. Like I say, you should have a month, maybe two. If you start to notice him getting worse before then, call me and we'll bring him back in. And if there's anything you want to ask me about, you can call me anytime."

He jots down a number on a scrap of paper and hands it to me.

"My home number," he says. "If I'm not in, leave a message and I'll get back to you. Don't be afraid to call."

Driving back to the lake, with the dog stretched out in the back seat, I think about how I'm going to break this to the kids. They'll be devastated. Kate, especially. She was six years old when we brought him home from the pound, an excitable, wriggling bundle of shiny black fur with a patch of white on his chest. Over the years as he got bigger, the patch moved slowly up to his chin, and he took up more and more space on Kate's bed, to the point where there was almost no room for her. We bought him his own bed, years ago, but he only lies in it when he thinks he's being punished.

When Kate first left for university, he went down to her room every night and automatically got on to her bed. He would lie there for an hour or so, then give up and come up to the third floor where David and I sleep, and scramble under our bed, where he'd stay until morning. Now and then he'd try sleeping with Adam, but my son has always been a restless sleeper. Once again, the dog would resign himself to burrowing under our bed where at least it was safe and there were no unexpected kicks from unconscious teenage boys.

At Christmas, and then again for a few weeks in the summer, Kate comes home from Montreal, and the dog picks up his old routine, obviously relieved to have things back to normal. When I think about Kate coming home to sleep alone, with no dog sharing her bed, the street ahead of me blurs.

✕ ✕ ✕

The telephone rings six or seven times in the small apartment my daughter shares with three other students. One of them, I think, is a boyfriend, but with Kate you're never sure. Not secretive, exactly, just selective about what she chooses to tell you. When she eventually answers the phone, she sounds tired. My parental reflexes hit immediate alert.

"Kate? Are you all right? It's me."

"Oh, hi, Mom. How are you?"

"You don't sound very well. Are you sick?"

"Just a late night. How're things out at the lake?"

"All right, I guess."

But my voice betrays me. Immediately *her* instincts are aroused and she wants to know what's the matter.

"Mom, are you okay? What's the matter, Mom? What happened?"

This is not how I've planned it. On the way back to the cabin, I came up with a speech about the natural order of things, and how animals befriend us and care about us and we love them. When it's time to let them go, we have the memory to carry with us always.

Instead, I've begun to cry, and I can't stop—I'm literally gasping for breath. Now Kate is truly alarmed, hearing her mother obviously in the middle of a breakdown thousands of miles away. It's not the dog; or at least, it's not *just* the dog—it's everything. When I can finally get my breath to speak, all I can tell my daughter is that I miss her. Which is true, but it's not her that I miss. I miss my babies because they are my youth; I miss what is gone and cannot be retrieved. There's a huge gaping hole in my heart where my old life used to be, and I can't believe I'll ever find anything as good to replace it.

"I miss you, too, Mom, but I'll see you at Christmas. Right? We're all getting together at Christmas. Aren't we?"

That final "aren't we," spoken after just a fraction of a pause, sounds so uncertain that I almost lose it all over again. Pulling myself together, I reassure my daughter that of course we will all be together at Christmas.

"I'm sorry, sweetie, I'm just feeling a little sad today. It's the weather—I forgot what it's like out here in November."

And then she asks me how the dog is, and I have no recourse but to tell her. I'm drained from crying, and so I just tell her what Dr. Jim told me—that the dog has cancer and probably only has another month or so to live.

"I'm sorry, Katie. I feel so bad having to tell you this. I know how you feel about him."

There's no response and I know she's crying. I have called my daughter up and made her cry and I can't reach out and comfort her. I absolutely hate this.

"Kate. Honey, I'm sorry. Don't cry." And then, "No, go ahead and cry. You cry all you want. He's a good dog, and we should cry over him."

Which sets me off again and for the next few minutes we cry and try to comfort each other over the phone.

"He's the best dog," she tells me. "The best dog in the whole world. He never hurt anybody, not even when Adam pulled his tail or wrestled too hard with him. All he would do is maybe growl just a little bit, but he'd never take even a little nip of a person. He's just the best."

She wants to know if he's in pain, and I explain that he gets tired easily, and he has some discomfort, but he's not in pain. Not yet.

"Will he be all right till Christmas?"

"Sweetie, I don't know."

"Mom, he has to be all right till Christmas. I have to say goodbye to him, you can't do anything until I see him."

"No, of course I won't. He'll be okay, Kate. You'll see him at Christmas."

"Promise?"

I promise, like I promised hundreds of times when she was small—promised to take her to a movie on Saturday if she was good at the dentist on Friday. Promised to be waiting right by the gate that first day of school in England. Promised to brush the tangles out of her hair without hurting her. All those promises made over the years, and I call myself a good mother because most of them were kept. Which is why she believes me this time: she knows that if my promise has any power at all, it will keep her dog alive for another six weeks.

Eventually, we say goodbye. At the last minute she wants to say goodbye to the dog. I take the phone over to where he is sleeping, lift up one silky, black ear, and place the receiver against his head for a moment. When I put the phone back to my own ear, she asks, "Did he know it was me, do you think?"

"His tail was wagging."

"I told him he's a good dog and that I'd be seeing him really soon."

"Take care, sweetie. Keep well."

"You, too. Take good care of him, Mom."

"I will."

After we say goodbye, I go to the book of quotations I keep with me, given to me years ago by Adam when it dawned on him his mother was a writer. It's there, by Francis Bacon:

"He that hath a wife and children hath given hostages to fortune; for they are impediments to great enterprises, either of virtue or mischief."

Change "wife" to "dog," and you have my life in a nutshell.

15

AT THE BEST OF TIMES THE LOCAL PAPER IS NOT heavy reading, and this is not the best of times. Two slim sections, with a page and a half devoted to "World News" and a kind of hodgepodge of local stories from all along the north shore of Lake Superior. The greatest amount of newsprint, in fact, appears to be devoted to the obituary pages which I always scan, out of a morbid curiosity. I'm looking for two things: how they died, and how old they were when they died. When they're seventy-five or older, I'm reassured—that makes sense, they got their three score and twenty, and then some. When they're my own age or younger, I feel slightly anxious, as if it could happen to me at any moment and I'm living on borrowed time.

The cause of death can be intriguing: "suddenly" can signify a suicide, especially if there's nothing at the bottom asking for donations to the Cancer Society or the Heart and Stroke Fund. The death of a child is always the worst; you torment yourself with the thought that this could have been your son or daughter. What guarantee do you have that their names won't be featured here, killed by a drunken driver or brought down by cancer or AIDS? When my thoughts head in this direction, I generally fold up the newspaper and go for a walk.

Today, there are no children, for which I am grateful. But in the far right column of the next-to-last page, I come across the following announcement:

SCARPONE: Raymond William Scarpone, age fifty-four years, of Thunder Bay, passed away unexpectedly at his residence on Wednesday, 5 November 1997.

The notice goes on to say that Ray was born in Hibbing, Minnesota, moved to the Lakehead in 1950, attended local schools and was a member of the Thunder Bay Musicians' Association, Local 591. He's survived by his mother, an older brother, and a niece. No wife. Ray never married.

Ray Scarpone was Tina's boyfriend the summer she lived at my father's. She was working as a cocktail waitress at a club called Drake's, named after the guy who owned it. Drake was a former drummer with a local heavy metal band; he found Jesus, gave up drinking, and opened a nightclub. His dream was to get out of the business altogether; he wanted to buy a church and become a preacher. He even had a church picked out in an old part of town where the congregation was dwindling and the place was practically bankrupt—he was just waiting for it to go on the market.

Originally, he planned to call his bar The Bleeding Lamb of God but his friends managed to convince him that a name like that wouldn't draw much of a crowd. Not in that town, anyway. Probably not anywhere. So he called it Drake's instead, but he tried to give the place a kind of religious atmosphere by sticking up signs like "Are You Ready to Meet Your Maker?" and "Born Again Means Salvation." Luckily, the people who came there didn't read a whole lot and if they did, life in the hereafter was not generally uppermost in their thoughts.

In spite of Drake's spiritual nature, or maybe because of it, his club was popular. He hired his former heavy metal buddies as the house band and brought in a bunch of young guys to fill in from time to time. The drinks were cheap, thanks to his decision that it was un-Christian to rip off his patrons, and he hired only the best-looking cocktail waitresses.

"Thy breasts are like two young roes that are twins," he told Tina when she went for the job, "which feed among the lilies."

She was flattered until she found out he'd been quoting from the Bible. The great thing about scripture, Drake liked to say, was that if you looked hard enough, you could find stuff to justify just about anything.

Ray Scarpone started off as one of the fill-in guitar players, but he was such a good singer Drake kept him on permanently. Tina thought he was beautiful. She thought he looked and sounded exactly like Paul McCartney and she wasted no time getting to know him; the very first night he played there she brought him back to her room at my father's place and they made exuberant love till about five in the morning. I know, because I was trying to sleep. It was stifling, even with the window open, and the heat of the bedroom, combined with the sound of Ray and Tina in the next room, made me feel like an actor with a bit part in a Tennessee Williams play.

Just as the sun was coming up, there was a knock at the door, and Tina came in, followed by Ray, who had a bath towel tied around his waist and a pair of Tina's flip-flops on his feet.

"This is Ray," she whispered. "Isn't he cute? Ray, meet my friend Alex."

"Hello, Alex," he said, keeping his towel in place with one hand and caressing Tina with the other.

"Ray has a couple of joints," Tina said. "Come join us."

For the next hour or so we smoked and listened to music. The dope was strong, and I was very tired. We lay down together on Tina's bed, getting stoned and laughing at just about everything.

Ray stroked Tina's hair and she laughed; he turned over and cupped my breasts in his hands, and I laughed. He made love to each of us, in turn, and when he finally collapsed, exhausted, she and I lay on either side of him, and smiled at each other.

"Not bad, huh?" she said.

"Not bad at all," I agreed.

"You have beautiful eyes," she said, reaching over and running a finger along my cheek.

"So do you. Wait a minute—haven't I seen you somewhere before? Weren't you on the cover of a national magazine?"

She laughed and leaned across Ray to kiss me, gently, on the cheek.

"Good night, Alex," she said. "Go to sleep."

"Good night, Tina. Sweet dreams."

We slept late, and when we awoke it was midday. Tina suggested we drive out to the falls.

"I want to cool off," she said. "And it's Sunday, so we don't have to work. Come with us, it'll be fun."

We drove out Highway 17 in Ray's 1965 Buick LeSabre, the three of us together in the front seat. The vinyl of the car seats stuck to our flesh, sweat formed under our breasts and between our thighs. Tina sat in the middle and rolled a joint. We passed it back and forth between us, finishing it just before we reached the turnoff to the park.

I remember the water level was low that summer, and in those days there were no protective barriers at the falls, just a small, iron railing that could easily be mounted. Ray said we should climb down the rocks to the bottom of the gorge. He'd done it all the time when he was a kid; he said there was nothing to it. Especially when the water was this low.

We parked the car, rolled another joint, and began to work our way down the rocks: Ray first, then Tina, then me. There was no path, and you had to watch where you stepped; it was slippery and steep. And it was noisy. The water thundered in our ears; our clothes were drenched from the mist.

When we reached the bottom, we hugged each other. Ray

pulled the joint from his shirt pocket but it was too wet to light. We found a small pool of water away from the falls, and Tina suggested we go for a swim but I demurred.

"I'm not a good swimmer," I said. "You go ahead."

She and Ray stripped off their clothes and waded into the water, which came up to their chins. The water was cold and they didn't stay in long; afterwards the three of us lay on the rocks and gazed at the hawks soaring above the falls.

"Ray," Tina said, rolling over on to her stomach, "be a good boy and give me a massage."

Obediently, Ray sat up and began gently kneading Tina's back. When she'd had enough, she told him to give me a massage, too, and he did.

"Good?" she asked me, when he was through.

Eyes closed, I nodded. "Good."

Who knows how long we might have stayed like that, had we not heard voices overhead. A family, come to the falls for a picnic, and the three of us half-naked on the rocks below. We pulled on our damp clothes and climbed back up the rocks; by the time we reached the top the intruders were nowhere to be seen.

"Do you think we shocked them?" Tina asked. She was pleased when I said yes, we probably had.

"I love to shock people," she said, sweetly. "It makes life less boring, don't you think?"

As we left the park, we passed an OPP cruiser, come to check us out, no doubt. Tina waved and blew the driver a kiss, and we headed back into town. Ray dropped us off, saying he had to go home to sleep. He was still living at home, apparently, but planned to get his own apartment soon. In the meantime, he'd be spending a great deal of time at my father's house.

The pattern that established itself that summer went like

Margie Taylor

this: three or four nights a week, Tina brought Ray home from work in the early hours of the morning, they made love, came to my room and woke me up, and we sat in bed smoking a joint and listening to music. Sometimes they went back to her room together, but usually they invited me to go with them. And I did. We were sharing Ray, Tina and I—I guess you could call it a threesome. Once, he suggested making love to me on my own, without Tina, but she didn't like that idea so he dropped it.

I didn't like it, either. The real attraction, for me, was having sex with Tina there. It wouldn't have been the same without her.

16

Since I came out to the lake in September, my days have developed a rhythm, a routine that has come to feel familiar, even comforting. They are bookended in the morning and evening by my walks with the dog, with the bulk of the day filled by long sessions on the computer. I chat with Adam or Kate at some point, usually just before bed, and once a week I drive into town for lunch with Joan, after which I stop at the supermarket and pick up the week's groceries. And every night, except for the time the power was off, I have a sauna.

The sauna is located at the back of the house, closer to the lake. Originally it must have been separate from the main building; now, though, a covered passageway links the two structures. The sauna contains a wood-burning stove filled with smooth, symmetrical stones gathered from the lake, a two-tiered pine bench, and an oblong shelf holding sweet-smelling soaps and a loofah. The original room has also been altered by the addition of a makeshift wall, creating a separate space to hang up your clothes and shower.

This is a real Finnish sauna, not one of those makeshift concoctions found in health clubs and hotels. Its basic design, or some variation of it, is found all along the lakefronts of northern Ontario. When Finns settled an area, they built their saunas first, often living in them until other rooms were added on, or a separate house was constructed. Civilized man could do without a living room and kitchen, perhaps, but not without a proper sauna.

Important things were carried out in the sauna, and getting clean was just one of them: babies were born here, wounds were healed, sore muscles were attended to after a day working out in the bush. Traditionally, whole families bathed together, relying on sweat and a birch whisk to stimulate the circulation; then finished with a dip in the lake or a roll in the snow, depending on the season.

This particular sauna has a painting on the wall—a group of happy Finns, all a little on the chubby side, are sharing a sauna together. An older woman, in the middle, holds a naked toddler on her lap; a young boy is about to douse himself with a bucket of water while his older sister leans forward to pick up a loofah. On the far right, an old man sits back against the wall, eyes closed, a beatific smile on his face. You can almost hear him thinking: Sweat. Great sweat. Life is good.

Nothing the least bit obscene about this scenario. Like the native North American sweat lodge, the sauna was sacred; to older Finns, having sex in a sauna would be like fornicating in church.

Of course, my generation was not overly troubled by matters of spiritual delicacy. Saunas were private, and their very nature required one to strip. They were, therefore, hotbeds of sexual activity. At a time when most sexual encounters took place in the back seat of a Chevy, saunas were a godsend.

I had had saunas before I met Tina; there was one in town not far from the university that was a favourite student hangout. But it wasn't until Tina came to stay at my father's place that I experienced a real old-fashioned sauna out at the lake.

It was Ray's idea, I think. It was a Sunday night and neither he nor Tina had to be at the club. Her tenants were away for the weekend and the place was empty.

We stopped at the general store on the highway east of town, to pick up hamburger meat and buns, and by the time we got to the lake it was after ten. The air was filled with the clamour of crickets and frogs and the rhythmic slapping of water against the rocks. As the sky slowly turned from blue to black, the stars appeared, one after another, right on cue.

While Ray got the fire going in the sauna, Tina and I sat up on the deck looking out over the lake, and drank beer. We didn't say much—she was particularly quiet that night, although she did remark at one point as to how she missed the lake and would be glad to get back out here in the fall.

I asked her why she rented the place out, if she didn't like living in town.

"I need the bread," she said, simply.

There was a silence; then, abruptly, she asked me what I thought of Ray.

"He's nice," I said, and she said, yes, she knew that, but what did I think of him as a lover?

"Is he any good?"

The question took me aback. "You should know," I said, "you sleep with him every night."

She shook her head and frowned. "I can't tell. Once I fall in love with a boy, I can't tell if he's any good or not. You tell me— what do you think? Is Ray good in bed or is he just average?"

I thought about it. "Well," I said, "I guess I'd say he's about average. No, better than average."

"Better than average." She thought about that for a moment. "So, on a scale of one to ten, where would he be?"

"Tina, for God's sake—"

But she persisted. "I want to know how you'd rate him on a scale of one to ten."

"So if one is—"

"One is so awful," she said, "you'd rather be ironing your father's underwear, and ten is so terrific you'd follow him to the ends of the earth."

Laughing, I told her I'd rate Ray as a seven, and she seemed satisfied. Ray came up and joined us on the deck, sparing me further analysis of his sexual prowess.

It was one of those northern August nights where the warmth of the day lingers long after the sun has set, and nothing feels more natural than sitting under the stars, drinking beer, and making desultory conversation. Nothing important is said, nothing significant happens, yet you remember those nights the rest of your life.

By the time the sauna was hot, we'd gone through the six-pack and smoked a significant amount of Ray's stash of home-grown. We stripped on the deck, and then made our way down to the water's edge in the dark, tripping and slipping into each other. The sauna was warm and welcoming, the stove glowing in the dark. Tina and I climbed up on to the pine bench, Ray shut the door and went to sit between us, but Tina shifted towards me so that she was in the middle instead.

It was a small, hot, dark space and there was not much room for the three of us. We leaned back and closed our eyes, letting the heat go to work on our bodies. There was no light, except for the small red glow at the base of the stove. Everything was heightened; I felt every touch of skin against skin, every minute drop of water.

Suddenly, I was overtaken by a wave of claustrophobia. I had to get out of there. I slid down from the bench and felt my way to the door. At first it wouldn't open; I pushed and it gave way unexpectedly. I stumbled outside, relieved to be out where I could see, out of the suffocating heat. I was standing a few feet from the sauna, willing my heart to stop pounding, when Tina joined me.

"It's the dope," she said. "Ray's homegrown is really strong. Are you okay?"

I nodded, but I wasn't okay. Everything was moving too quickly; I couldn't breathe.

"Come on," she said, taking me by the hand, "we'll go for a swim and cool off."

"I'm not a good swimmer, remember?"

"It's okay," she said, leading me down to the water, "it's shallow for a long way out. We'll just paddle around and get the sweat off."

I've never trusted dark water—not being able to see to the bottom, not knowing what might be floating there. But my skin was overheated, my body was longing for a cool, refreshing dip, so I followed her into the lake.

The relief, as the waters moved up my body, calming me, inviting me to sink down into the slow, sleepy motion of the waves. My fear dissipated, I could feel it leaving my body, feel the therapeutic movement of the water lifting me up, holding me. Protecting me. I turned on my back and floated, and the stars were closer than I'd ever seen them before. The night was tangible; I felt the darkness move around me like a living creature.

Ray swam by me. "Are you all right?" he asked.

When I said I was fine, absolutely fine, he laughed and said it was powerful dope.

"It's not the dope," I said. "It's the water."

He laughed again and swam further out. Tina came up beside me and held out her hand.

"Come on," she said, "let's swim together."

And so, very gently, she pulled me out further, keeping hold of my hand until the water was over our heads and we were floating together in the darkness, looking up at the stars.

After a while, we heard Ray calling to us. We turned around and began paddling back to the shore. When the water was shallow enough to stand and walk, she turned to me and said,

"My tenants are leaving at the end of the month. Will you come out and stay with me?"

"For how long?"

She smiled. "For as long as you want."

"What about Ray?"

"What about Ray?" she said. "He'll be here too, some of the time. You don't mind, do you?"

I told her I'd think about it.

※ ※ ※

At the end of the summer, Tina moved out. She called me from the lake and I hitchhiked out there every weekend that fall. Sometimes Ray gave me a lift; sometimes he was working in town and I went on my own. When he was with us, the three of us slept together; when she and I were on our own, we sat up late, listening to music, drinking Southern Comfort, and I fell asleep on the couch.

That last night—the night we talked about Janis Joplin— that was the night I told her about David. He was my third year psychology prof. Although I'd only spoken to him once or twice outside the classroom, I knew I was falling in love with him. I told Tina that, and she said I should bring him out to the lake.

"Out here?" I said, and she said, yes, why not?

"I couldn't, Tina. Anyway, I'm pretty sure he's married. And he's British and very proper. I don't think he's ever smoked dope. He'd be very uncomfortable."

This offended her; when I saw that, I tried to explain myself, but I just made it worse. We lapsed into an uncomfortable silence. When I awoke the next morning I decided to leave without waking her. I walked up to the main road, stuck out my thumb and got a lift into town with a hydro repairman. I meant to call her after that, but I didn't. I got busy with school, and David and I began having coffee together two or three times a week. Eventually, he told me he was leaving his wife.

"For me?" I asked, hoping that wasn't the case.

He smiled and shook his head. "For me," he said. "But you probably have something to do with it."

David moved into his own apartment a week later, and we began living together. Every now and then Tina's name would come up in conversation and I'd tell myself I should give her a call, just to see how she was. Somehow, though, I never got around to it.

17

W HEN I TELL JOAN I'M PLANNING A TRIP TO
St. Andrew's Cemetery, she immediately offers to come.

"I love cemeteries," she says. "Mind you, I don't know that I
could spend a night in one, the way Vicky Ternetti did. She was
a tough old bat, even back then."

She suggests we take her car, and as we head out on Oliver
Road, she tells me Tina was buried in St. Andrews's too, originally. Right next to Conrad.

"Her mother kept saying they were star-crossed lovers—like
Romeo and Juliet. She wanted them to be buried together. The
Schaeffers finally gave in and then a few months later Tina's
mom came back to town and had her dug up."

"Why on earth would she do that?"

Joan shakes her head. "I'm not sure. Apparently she went
out to the gravesite and there were footprints in the snow, all over
where Tina was buried. She thought people were showing disre-
spect for her daughter, trampling on her memory. But I think the
footprints were from Vicky camping out there at Christmas.
Anyway, she was determined to have Tina moved and in the end
that's what happened."

"Where did they move her to?"

"Toronto, probably. And then Marianne, Tina's sister, died
and I guess she buried her there, too. Both her daughters, dead
within a year. Pretty sad, when you think of it."

I have a file of old newspaper clippings, dating back to the
weekend Tina died—the weekend of a huge downpour, the
worst storm in Thunder Bay's history. Roads were washed out,
basements were flooded, and the rain pelted down for twenty-

four hours. The waters of the Kaministiquia River spilled over their banks, trees were uprooted, and hydro poles were toppled.

The same paper carries a card of thanks from Conrad's family, two weeks after his death: "We would like to extend and express our sincere thanks," it says, "to all our friends for their thoughtfulness shown to us in our recent loss of our dear son and beloved brother, Conrad." And then, just two columns over, there is this, under Deaths:

> *Erika Kristina Van Buren, age thirty-two years, of 6 Grandview Ave., Grandview Beach, died at her residence 10 September 1977. Born in Germany, she had resided in Thunder Bay for the past ten years. She was a graduate of Lakehead University.*

Her mother and sister are mentioned. It's short and sad. And there is nothing else, nothing that I've ever been able to find, either in the local paper or anywhere else, that gives any more information. Nothing about how she died, nothing about an inquest or any kind of inquiry into her death. Case closed.

This stretch of road is pretty bleak, especially at this time of year. The trees stand naked in the wind, stark against a dull grey sky. All those years on the coast have washed away memories of the mind-numbing cold, the wretched wind that pierces your chest and captures your breath if you're stupid enough to try to breathe without a scarf or glove over your mouth.

"I forgot about this," I say, and Joan nods; she seems to know what I mean.

"Not very Hollywood at the moment, is it? I guess you'll be glad to get back to the coast."

"Actually, I'm thinking about not going back."

Why would I say that? Until the moment I open my mouth, the thought has not even occurred to me. Yet, once said, I know it's true; I'm thinking about leaving David, getting a place of my own. Starting over.

"Is that what you want?"

"I don't know. But it's the best I can come up with at the moment."

"Maybe you should talk to David about it first. Let him have some input in this."

"David's had nothing but input in my life for twenty-five years, Joan. I think maybe I need to start making decisions myself."

We drive on for a moment in silence; then Joan pulls over to the side of the road.

"Did I ever tell you I'm a Baha'i?" she asks, after putting the car into park. "I guess I should say I *was* a Baha'i, when I was younger. I've kind of lapsed over the years, but I believe in the basic principles. If I was ever going to get religious again, that'd be the religion I'd choose."

"Joan, are you about to try to convert me?"

She smiles and carries on. "The Baha'is have this thing called a year of patience. If a couple chooses to divorce, they have to live apart for a year, but continue to try to work things out. Then, when the year is up, if they can't resolve things, the divorce becomes final. I think you and David should have a year of patience."

"Is that what you and Jimmy did?" Jimmy was Joan's second husband—she'd had a least two. I'd got the impression he was a kind of Mafioso; it was Jimmy who gave her the snake ring.

"Lord, no. Jimmy was many things, but he was not one for being patient—not even for a month, let alone a year. I did try it with my first husband, but it didn't work. But I still think it's a good idea—in theory, anyway. I just wanted to mention it."

I admit that it does sound interesting, but it's not really relevant, for David and me. After all, we're not talking about divorcing—we're not talking about anything.

"Well, if you do," she says, "will you promise at least to think about it?"

I promise and Joan seems satisfied. She puts the car back into gear, and we continue out to the cemetery.

✠ ✠ ✠

The sign in the window of the small office says "Closed," but Joan says not to worry, she's sure she can find the burial spot.

"I haven't been out here in years," she says, "but this is the older part—it hasn't changed much."

She leads me along a path that winds past a semicircle of small white gravestones, each marking the place where a soldier lies. Several of those stones are decorated with wreaths, probably placed there in honour of Remembrance Day. My general inclination is to linger in these places, but Joan is marching on ahead, and I have to hurry to keep up with her. Besides, on a day like this, it's too cold for lingering.

She turns and calls back to me: "It's not far from here, I'm sure of that. I think it's just a little past this fountain."

Another hundred steps and we've found it, a black granite marker next to an identical tombstone, set back just a little from the road. One for Conrad and one for his stepfather, who died ten years later. Conrad's is adorned with a photograph, an Old Country practice, I think; there are a lot of graves here displaying faded pictures of the deceased. He would have turned thirty that year; the photo shows a handsome young man in a black shirt and light-coloured jacket, his hair slightly tousled, falling across his forehead. Dark, well-defined eyebrows call attention to his eyes, which are watchful, alert. He has the look of a young animal on guard. Underneath, the inscription reads:

In loving memory of a dear father, son and brother,
Conrad Schaeffer 1947—1977

I've brought my camera with me, and snap a few pictures of the tombstone. A good-looking guy—easy to see what Tina saw in him.

"His mom would have more pictures of him," Joan suggests. "I could give Nadine a call, see if she'd talk to you. See if her mother would meet you."

"I don't know. I hate the thought of causing an old lady any kind of pain—why would she want to talk to a stranger about the death of her son?"

"In my experience," Joan says, "mothers always want to talk about their children, even after they're dead. She's a sweet lady. Her English isn't very good, but you could get Nadine to help you."

And so we agree that she will call Conrad's sister, try to arrange a meeting. As we leave the cemetery, I feel a little uneasy; the more I find out about Conrad Schaeffer, the harder it'll be to write about him. That's the problem with facts: they tend to get in the way of the story.

18

"DO YOU THINK IT'S POSSIBLE THAT HE'S ACTUALLY
fallen in love with you?"

I'm attempting to balance a tray of cookies and a teapot and
avoid tripping over the dog, who has settled himself squarely at
the feet of Dr. Jim Bennett and refuses to be lured away, even
with the promise of a treat. He rests his muzzle on the vet's
knees and gazes adoringly upwards, his eyes half closed in the
ecstasy of having his ears rubbed. Dr. Jim laughs and gives the
dog a quick squeeze, then takes the tray and sets it down on the
coffee table.

"He's a great dog," he tells me, and then, to the dog, "Yes,
you're a good old boy, aren't you? And you're doing just fine."

The dog threw up last night, all over the living room rug.
I'm ashamed to admit I used that as an excuse to call the number Dr. Jim gave me. He, in turn, suggested coming out this
afternoon to check out the situation. I protested, at first—said
I'd bring the dog into town, instead. But Jake was refusing to
leave the house, let alone get into the car, and when the doctor
said it was a beautiful day for a drive, he'd be happy to come
out—well, of course I gave in.

"Do you really think he's doing fine?" I ask. "I mean,
there's no chance the x-rays were wrong?"

The look he gives me dispels all hope for a minor miracle.

"No, I'm afraid not. The blood tests confirmed the diagno-
sis. I'm sorry."

Then, because I make no attempt to hide my disappointment, he says in a more cheerful voice, "But you're doing a terrific job of keeping him as healthy as possible. His coat is shiny,

his eyes are clear, and he's not in any pain. Throwing up last night must've just been something he ate. Labs get into all kinds of garbage; they'll eat anything. They're the goats of the dog world."

The vet is seated in the middle of the sofa; I'm perched rather gingerly on the edge of a chair I don't normally use, an egg-shaped concoction of moulded plastic and aluminum that I've always thought belongs in the Smithsonian. I've yet to work out what it's doing in this otherwise comfortable, even rustic, summer house. A gift from someone, perhaps, or an objet d'art purchased on the spur of the moment and too expensive to throw away. I pour us each a cup of tea and hold out the sugar bowl and creamer. Dr. Jim spoons three large helpings of sugar into his cup, ignores the milk, and explains, with a smile, "My weakness. Got a sweet tooth."

"Mine's chocolate."

"Milk chocolate or the deep, dark kind?"

"The deeper and darker the better," I tell him, and his grin spreads right across his face—he has absolutely the best smile of any man I know. To distract myself from concentrating on my visitor's mouth, I bring the conversation back to the dog.

"So you don't think he's in any pain?"

"Absolutely not. You saw the way he bounced over to me when I walked in the door? There's no way he'd be moving that quickly if he was hurting. Would you, boy? No, you would not."

The dog emits a deep, throaty groan of pleasure and submits once again to the caress of the vet. I find I'm staring at that well-shaped hand, the fingers kneading the muscles in the side of the dog's head. What would it feel like to have those fingers prodding my own muscles, I wonder? They look knowledgeable, as if they'd know exactly where the pain was located, and how to make it disappear.

"Have a cookie," I suggest, pushing the plate of Girl Guide cookies over to his side of the table.

"Thanks," he says. "I haven't had these in years."

"I'll give you a box to take home when you leave. I shouldn't even be eating them. And when I'm writing, it's deadly. I can eat an entire box in one sitting, and not even realize it."

"So how's the book going? About your friend, the one who was murdered?"

"You've got a good memory."

"Actually, this kind of stuff is a hobby of mine. Before I decided to go into veterinary practice, I worked in a coroner's office for a while, in Windsor."

"What made you change your mind?"

He grins and gives the dog an affectionate pat on the head. "I guess it just seemed like more fun helping animals get better than signing death certificates for humans."

Looking around the small, comfortable room with its wall hangings and watercolour paintings, he says, "You've done this place up really nice—I'm impressed."

"In that case, I'd better come clean: almost nothing in here belongs to me, except for a few books and photos and all that paperwork. And the laptop, of course—everything else was here when I arrived."

I wish I hadn't admitted it; it'd be nice to be seen as a person who collects things, who makes things homey and pleasant. He grins and tells me he's relieved to hear it. "You told me you'd been here for a couple of months—I figured you must be some kind of superwoman to get the place looking like this in that time."

"I wish. No one could ever call me a superwoman, that's for sure."

"Just as well. I married one. It took me five years to realize

Margie Taylor

that what she really wanted was a guinea pig, not a husband."

There is a pause and I offer him another cookie.

"So this friend of yours—was she murdered?"

"I'm not sure, but I just can't believe it was suicide."

"Was there an autopsy?"

"No, and no one was charged with her death. But her face was blown off. She was supposed to have put a gun to her forehead and pulled the trigger. I just can't imagine her choosing that way to die. She'd have taken pills, or slit her wrist. Something that wouldn't have destroyed her face."

"She'd have wanted to be a beautiful corpse."

"Exactly. But how do you prove that? How do you prove it wasn't suicide?"

"Well." Dr. Jim takes a bite of cookie and considers the question. "First of all, you'd need some evidence of a struggle. You know, did she put up a fight? That'd be the first thing."

It occurs to me to tape-record this. The doctor agrees, and waits while I set up the machine on the coffee table and make sure the batteries are working. Then, I go into interview mode:

"What might you see, if there had been a struggle?"

"Grip marks, for one thing. Bruises on the upper arms— what they call restraining marks, where you can see where she's been tied up. Or maybe there's some evidence that before they killed her, they knocked her out, rendered her unconscious so they didn't have to tie her up. But that can be a hard thing to prove."

"Why?"

"Well, the difficulty is that if you're smart, and experienced, and you've done this kind of thing before, you confine the assault to the head, okay? So you hit her over the head with a baseball bat or something, knock her out, and then you blow her brains out with a shotgun to cover up the blow to the head."

He relates this all quite cheerfully, helping himself to another cookie.

"It can be the perfect crime, if you think about it. Because in most suicide investigations nobody checks the fingerprints on the trigger. All that happens is they check if she had a long enough reach to do this, to blow her brains out. I mean, if it was a criminal investigation, the police labs would do residue testing on the hands but that's only done if somebody raises suspicions. Otherwise it's treated as a routine suicide—it's not a suspicious death until somebody raises the alarm, either the coroner or the police or maybe a family member."

Dr. Jim is becoming quite animated.

"You know, this is interesting stuff," he says. "Maybe I should have gone in for coroner after all. Although you don't actually get a lot of training to be one, you know. Most of them are just family doctors or emergency physicians or whatever, out in the regions. If there's anything really suspicious, a murder or something, it gets referred to the head guy in Toronto."

"You mentioned about Tina having a long enough reach to shoot herself. What does her reach have to do with it?"

"Well, now. You need to know the kind of gun that was used. For one thing, it can be sawn-off and secondly, some of the different calibres aren't as long as others. You take some of the four-tens, which is the smaller calibre one, they're actually quite petite, they're sort of the size of a .22—most people have the ability to reach the trigger on that, when the barrel's in their mouth. With the so-called goose guns, the longer guns, you generally find that the guy—I say 'guy' because 90 per cent of suicides like this are men—the guy's got his sock off so he can use his toe. Or maybe he's used a fishing rod rest. So there's a means by which he can reach the trigger.

"Most people," he continues, "use .22s or shorter guns. If

people are using big 12-gauge shotguns that have a barrel that's longer than their arms—and especially if it's a woman—well, then they'd have to find an extra means of getting there. And that's what the police would look for."

I tell him that, for a vet, he knows a lot about guns. He grins and says it was his dad—he took him hunting when he was a kid.

"He grew up in the outdoors, and he thought kids should know their way around a gun."

"Do you still hunt?"

"Jesus, no."

He seems shocked by the question, says no one dedicated to healing animals would deliberately go out and shoot them.

"I never liked it," he says, "even back then. I used to have nightmares for weeks afterwards about deer and dead rabbits."

That, somehow, is reassuring. The more I talk to this Dr. Jim person the more I like him. Forcing myself to get back to the subject, I tell him that what I want to know is how you'd go about finding out, twenty years after the fact, whether or not a person was murdered. Dr. Jim rubs his chin, ponders, takes another sip of coffee.

"Well, there'd be a coroner's file, of course. Which might not say much, it might be pretty skimpy, depending on what they were thinking at the time—"

"I've applied for that," I tell him. "I can't have it. They won't show it to anybody except her family and from what I can find out, her family's all dead."

"All of them?"

I explain that there was only Tina, her half-sister Marianne, and her mother; her sister died a year after she did, and her mother's been dead for quite a while now. There was a stepfather once upon a time, but nobody has any idea what happened to him. "He's probably dead now too, when you think about it—he'd be in his eighties if he was alive."

"Yeah, that makes sense." He takes a sip of his coffee and absent-mindedly helps himself to another cookie. "I guess you're pretty well out of luck there all right."

"But if somebody dies like that, with a gunshot wound to the head, wouldn't there automatically be an autopsy? And wouldn't that be on file somewhere?"

"I doubt it. Most coroners autopsy maybe half of the bodies that get referred to them. And they generally only do an autopsy if they need to determine the cause of death. So a shooting or a hanging, or a carbon monoxide poisoning, maybe, those are the kinds of things they'd autopsy. And if a person's older, over seventy or something, they don't usually do an autopsy at all. I mean, say the guy's had a history of high blood pressure, he was overweight and he smoked, well, there's really no need to look any further."

"Do people—family members—ever push for an autopsy when the doctor doesn't want to do one? Have you ever known that to happen?"

"Oh sure, all the time. They do it with their animals, too. I've got an elderly lady right now who's demanding I operate on her cat and find out if her next-door neighbour poisoned it. Poor old thing."

"The cat or the old lady?"

"Well, both of them, I guess. But I was referring to the old lady. The cat was nineteen years old and about twenty pounds overweight—believe me, that's one animal that died of natural causes."

"So will you do it anyway, even though you don't think it's necessary?"

"I guess I will if she insists. Problem is, it won't end there.

If I find nothing she won't believe me. What she really needs is another cat. Which is what I've suggested to her."

The dog shifts in his sleep as if all this talk of death and dying upsets him. I'd like to suggest we go into another part of the room to continue our conversation but of course, the doctor would think I was nuts. And the dog would get up and follow us anyway.

"And what about the other way—when the doctor wants to do an autopsy and the family, the widow or whatever, they don't?"

He grins. "We bully them. Well, the doctor does. It sounds awful, I know, but there are all kinds of ways of persuading people to go along with it. You explain to them how difficult it might be if they get an undetermined death certificate, problems with insurance, lots of other things. You point out to them the legal situation. And you reassure them, too. You explain you do not cut people's faces up, you don't dice them into little cubes of meat; they'll get the body back pretty much as it was before. Some people have religious objections, but there's nothing written into Islamic or Jewish law that says an autopsy can't be performed. Not in Canada, anyway. So people generally resign themselves to it, and the doctors do it and that's that."

The cookie plate is empty. I offer to refill it but Dr. Jim says no, he'd better not. We sit in silence for a moment, the late afternoon sun filtering through the window like a benediction.

"I love this part of the world," he says, with a nod to the view beyond the glass. "I came here six years ago, when my marriage split up. I figured it'd be a good place to get over things—kind of a temporary refuge. And now I can't imagine living anywhere else."

That happens to people, I say. They come for a short while and stay forever. Or they grow up here, like me, and keep making plans to return.

"I never felt I belonged here," I confess, feeling suddenly comfortable with this man I barely know. "I grew up wanting to be in London, or Paris. I couldn't wait to get out of here. And I still don't really want to be here. It's like there's some part of me here I left behind, and I can't be a whole person without it."

The doctor nods as if he knows exactly what I mean. "For me it was a case of finding a place that fit. I was a square peg everywhere else; here I just fit."

"You're lucky. Lots of people never find that."

The doctor glances at his watch and tells me he's sorry, he didn't realize it was getting late; he's going to have to get going. Which is my cue to clear my throat and suggest he might like to stay to supper—I don't realize, until I begin to speak, that I've had this idea in the back of my mind for the past hour. It's just been so pleasant sitting here with this man, discussing an admittedly gruesome topic, noting the way his jawline forms a kind of muted W when he smiles. His voice, too, is attractive, like the sound of soft gravel beneath your feet.

Stop it, Alex. For God's sake—haven't you learned anything from what happened last year? And the answer comes back: What I have learned is that I retain the capacity for sex. And unfortunately, once learnt, it's difficult to forget.

For a moment he looks as if he might accept the dinner invitation, but what he says is, "That would be great, but I promised Morgan I'd make it back in time for the early show. We belong to the film club at the university—apparently tonight we're seeing some kind of Japanese remake of *It's a Wonderful Life*."

Oh. Morgan. "So Morgan is your—"

I end the sentence on an up note and Dr. Jim finishes it for me. "Partner," he says. "We've been together for almost five years."

So. He *is* married, after all. Brightly, to cover my disappointment, I remark that Morgan is an unusual name for a woman, but that I'd always wanted to name my daughter Morgan, after my grandfather.

"My husband talked me out of it, though. He didn't think it was very feminine."

Another smile, and he corrects me: "Well, actually, my Morgan"—and there's just a hint of emphasis on the "my"—"is a man. He teaches forestry at the university."

"Oh. Right. I see."

My surprise must be obvious, because he goes on to say, "I assumed you knew I was gay—it's such a small town, everyone seems to know everybody's business."

Now I do manage to paste a chirpy little smile on my face.

"Oh, well, I don't get out much."

He laughs.

"Neither do I, except to these monthly film showings. If I don't get a move on I'll miss that, too, and there'll be hell to pay."

He stands up and as he reaches for his jacket he remembers something. "You know, if you've run up against a brick wall finding out about your friend, you might want to talk to someone who knew the boyfriend."

"I did. I talked to an old girlfriend of his. And a friend of mine is trying to arrange a meeting with his mother and sister."

"Well, I guess you've covered all the bases."

As I walk him to the door, the dog gets up and follows right behind, as if he expects to go along, too.

"See? What did I tell you? He's crazy about you."

Dr. Jim kneels down into a crouching position and ruffles the dog affectionately behind the ears.

"It's okay, boy," he tells him, "you'll be fine. Get out and chase a rabbit or two, that'll make you feel better."

And what, I wonder, will make me feel better? Rabbits sure as heck won't do it, although I smile and wave cheerfully from the open doorway as he backs out of the driveway.

"Thank you," I call out, as he smiles and waves back. "Thanks for coming out." He rolls down his window. "Thanks for the cookies," he says, holding up the box I've given him out of my kitchen stash. "Call me if you need anything."

And he's gone. The dog looks positively bereft; I know just how he feels.

19

Joan calls the following morning to say she spoke with Nadine, Conrad's sister. The Schaeffers have agreed to see me.

"I told her you used to write for the paper," Joan says. "I said you had a parenting column. She doesn't read the papers and she's never heard of you. But she said her mom has lots of pictures of Conrad and they all liked Tina, although they thought she was a little weird in the end. How's your shorthand?"

"Why?"

"Nadine doesn't want to be taped. She says you can take notes, if you want, but she doesn't want you to bring a tape recorder. I said it wouldn't be a problem."

"My shorthand is non-existent, but I can take notes. I may not be able to read them afterwards, but I can take them."

"Speaking of taking notes," she says, "I've been thinking about you and David. Have you thought about writing him a letter? Sometimes it's easier if you put things down on paper."

I'm not much of a letter writer; when I tell Joan that, she finds it amusing.

"You wrote a national newspaper column three times a week. It's what you do."

"That was different. I was writing to deadline. There aren't any deadlines when it comes to writing letters, so I don't write them."

In all the years we've been together, I've never written anything to David longer than a note. "Kate's at the Andersons', Adam's at soccer. Can you put the potatoes on at 5:30? I'll be home at 6." If I'd kept all the correspondence from our years together it would amount to a catalogue of errands, schedules, chores. The marriage is in the details.

✄ ✄ ✄

As luck would have it, David calls that evening, just after I get in from walking the dog. I've put a pot of water on the stove and am sitting by the window, waiting for it to boil.

"I was just thinking about you," I say. "I was thinking of writing you a letter."

"Why would you want to do that? Why not just pick up the phone and call me?"

"I was thinking about something that happened years ago. I was remembering—"

Feeling suddenly foolish for bringing it up, I stop; he prods me to continue.

"I was remembering that ski trip Kate took, the time we thought she was lost."

"She was in grade six."

"You remember." I can't keep the surprise out of my voice. It was such a small thing, really, and it was over so quickly.

"Of course I remember," David says. "She'd gone skiing with her class, up Mount Seymour. They were supposed to get back to the school by five, and she wasn't on the bus. You went to meet her and all the children got off the bus and Katie wasn't there. I'd just got home, and I remember I didn't take my coat off. I just stood there, and you said, 'What should we do?' And I didn't know."

"I've been thinking—that's the only time I've ever seen you afraid."

"Forty-five minutes," he says. "It seemed much longer than that."

Margie Taylor

In the confusion and excitement of the day, Kate had missed the bus and got a ride back with a friend's parent. But for almost an hour we thought she'd gone missing. We pictured the bleak darkness of the mountain at night, and our daughter out there, lost, alone, possibly in pain. The fear in David's eyes that night, and the relief when she walked through the front door—flushed from the snow and exercise, completely oblivious to the panic she'd caused us—were not emotions I'd seen in him before.

Now he asks, "Why would you think I'd forget something like that?"

"I don't know. It was such a long time ago, I guess."

"You sound sad."

"Do I? I guess I am. November's such a horrible month. It's either cloudy skies and rain or freezing cold and snow. Either way, it's depressing."

"It'll be Christmas in just over a month. That'll cheer you up."

Christmas. "Actually, David, I'm thinking about not coming home for Christmas."

There's a pause; I can only imagine how he's taking this. I can almost see him rubbing his hand slowly back and forth across his chin, the way he used to do in class when he was trying to work out how to answer a particularly complex question. Before he can respond, I add that I may not be coming home at all—at least, not for a while.

"Why is that?"

"Well, I have more people to talk to, for one thing. If I come home at Christmas I'd only have to come back again next spring, so I thought I might as well stay here and get it done."

"What about the children?" he asks. "It wouldn't be a very nice Christmas for them if you weren't there." Or for me, either—that's what I'm waiting for him to say. But he doesn't.

"The children aren't children anymore, David. They're all grown up, and they're coming home to be with their friends, not us. Kate will be home for exactly ten days. Adam just might be able to spare a week before he rushes back to fabulous California. Believe me, it will not be a big deal."

"You really are sad," he says, as if he's only just realized it. "I'm sorry, Alex. What can I do?"

"Nothing."

"Write me that letter, will you?" he says.

"The water's boiling, David. I have to go."

20

"PILLS AND ALCOHOL KILLED MY BROTHER. I DON'T care what the inquest decided."

Nadine Schaeffer makes this declaration while chain-smoking cigarettes and guiding me through the family photo album. Nadine, her mother, Klara, her younger brother, Leo, and I are gathered around the kitchen table, in the house near the coal docks where Conrad grew up. Nadine was two years younger than her brother. She says she's the one who knew him best.

Leo sits next to me, listening intently to the conversation, nodding or shaking his head as the situation arises. He can't speak properly but he's exuberantly friendly and makes himself understood by sheer persistence. I've found a far more welcoming group than I expected.

Nadine wants me to know, right away, that she thinks the coroner's report was a crock. The autopsy on Conrad was ordered by the insurance company that held the policy on the camp he bought, the one out near Tina's. It found no sign of pills or drugs of any kind in Conrad's system. There was a lot of liquor, but the doctor said what killed him was that his lungs collapsed and he couldn't breathe.

"I still don't believe it," Nadine says. "We all knew how many pills he was taking—it was no secret. I just don't get it."

Her mother isn't so sure. "Remember how sick he was when he was a baby?" she says. "He was so sick—my God, we thought he would die."

Nadine explains this was when they were living in the garage, the first winter they came to Canada.

"Mom took him to emergency in the middle of the night—

she had to walk there, with little Conrad all wrapped up in blankets. There was no bus and she couldn't afford to call an ambulance. They kept him in the sick kids' ward for two weeks; they weren't sure he was going to make it. I wasn't born yet, but I heard the story all my life."

Klara makes the sign of the cross.

"He was very bad, even your father was afraid. After that, when he got better, I never put him down. The rest of that winter, I carried him everywhere."

"Mom was always afraid something was going to happen to Conrad. Every time he caught a cold, she thought it was going to turn into pneumonia. She was a real worrywart, weren't you, Mom?"

Her mother shrugs her shoulders, as if to say, Mothers are like that; what can I say?

Nadine turns a page in the album and points to a black and white photo of a fair-haired young man in a German army uniform.

"This is my favourite photo of my father," Nadine says. "Doesn't he look handsome? I wish I'd known him when he was young."

"How did he die?" I ask. "If you don't mind talking about it."

Nadine pauses to light another cigarette from the stub of the first.

"The war destroyed him," she says. "All those things that happened to the men, they couldn't talk about it when they got home. And Germany lost, which was terrible for my dad. I think he felt ashamed, you know what I mean? And angry. When he was drinking, he'd say Germany had gone to the dogs. He didn't like the country filling up with DPs. And then we came to Canada, and he was a DP too."

"Everyone is poor here, in Canada," Klara says, and her daughter corrects her:

"Was poor, Mom. Everyone *was* poor."

"Is not shameful to be poor, but Rudy doesn't think like that," her mother continues. "He doesn't see that here there is future."

"That was the difference between Canada and the old country," Nadine explains. "Being poor was how you started life here; it wasn't how you ended it. And you could live pretty well on almost nothing. Mom always had a vegetable garden out back, and there'd always be some neighbour who'd gone out and shot a deer, and they'd share the meat. You might be poor but you didn't have to starve."

According to Nadine, her father grew increasingly morose and bitter about life in Canada; in Germany, he'd been a man with respect. People had laughed at his jokes and he looked down on the refugees who were taking jobs away from good German men. Now he saw himself at the very bottom of the barrel—only the Indians were worse off, and they didn't care. He was one of thousands of immigrants in this country: Slavs, Poles, Ukes, Wops, Krauts. He was German, but to the ignorant Canadians he was just another Displaced Person. He'd come to this country of his own free will, had paid for his passage and that of his family. Never had he even seen inside one of those refugee camps, full of stinking Jews and Polaks. Yet here in this so-called promised land, he was labeled a DP every time he opened his mouth. That was the real crime of losing the war, that he and others like him should be good for nothing but shovelling shit for the railway.

And so he drank and nursed his grievances; everyone was against him. One summer morning, after a night spent drinking alone down at the wharf, with only the rats for company,

Rudy Schaeffer, husband of Klara and father of Bridget, Nadine, and Conrad, went home and hanged himself in the basement of this very house. It was 13 August 1961, the day the East German government chose to seal off East from West Berlin.

"My mother worked hard all her life," Nadine tells me. "She's Old Country, you know what I mean? Life is tough, then you die. When my father died, she married my stepdad, had three more kids, and got on with it. She didn't sit around feeling sorry for herself."

Klara pours out more coffee, offers a slice of cake, and the conversation turns to Tina.

"I liked her a lot," Nadine says. "She was sweet, and she had such a good sense of humour. And the two of them, they looked so good together."

Was Conrad in love with her?

"Absolutely. He was crazy about her, there was never any doubt in my mind about that. My brother loved her very much."

Klara agrees that her son was in love but says she worried about him: worried about the friends he hung out with, the narcotics officers who came around asking questions. Conrad told her not to talk to them, but it was hard for her—she was from the Old Country; the police frightened her.

She worried, too, about his business deals. Conrad had a lot of business deals that summer, on his way to the one big deal that would set him up for life. He was planning to make a lot of money and then take Tina to Mexico to live. Or Spain. Somewhere warm where the food was cheap and the drugs were plentiful.

But the plans changed all the time. One minute he was talking about heading south, or to Europe. And then he went and bought himself that camp out on the lake, the one Herbie Sutherland was going to help him renovate. They never finished it; somehow, Conrad never found the time.

Money, though—they had plenty of that. His mother recalls the time Tina came by to give her a lift to a doctor's appointment. As Klara got into the car, she noticed an envelope in the back seat, stuffed with money. Crisp new one hundred dollar bills spilled out of the top; it was indecent, she thought, to have all that money lying around like it was garbage.

Tina said the money was Conrad's, she was hanging on to it for him. Klara shook her head.

"I don't like," she told Tina. "Is not good, driving around like that. What are you thinking?"

Two days later, when Conrad dropped by the house for something to eat, she asked him about the money in the car. Business, he said. Don't worry about it, Ma, it's just business.

"Busy-ness," she says now, shaking her head. "What is busy-ness when you don't be working, you don't do nothing? What is, I ask you?"

According to Nadine, he and Tina fought a lot that summer. Conrad was drinking too much, taking too many pills. And then Elvis died.

Nadine doesn't subscribe to the theory that her brother killed himself because of Elvis. But she admits that in the week following Elvis's death, Conrad seemed to get worse. And then he collapsed out at the lake, and Tina called the ambulance.

"The doctors wanted him to stay there," Nadine says. "They said his heart had stopped beating and they wanted to run some tests. But he wouldn't. Maybe if he'd stayed in the hospital, my brother would still be alive." At this point, Nadine's version of events differs from what Vicky told me. Nadine says Conrad checked himself out of the hospital and took a cab to his mother's. Klara ran him a bath and cooked him some soft-boiled eggs. ("He don't eat too much back then," she remembers. "Not very hungry.")

*dis*placed PERSONS

In the meantime, a bunch of Conrad's friends had turned up at Nadine's place, and by mid-afternoon there were maybe a dozen people in her downtown apartment, drinking and popping amphetamines. One of the guys called Conrad and told him to come by, join the party. Tina was expecting him back at the lake but he said he'd drop in for an hour or so. He finished eating, called a cab, and waited on the living room sofa, where he could see the street through the front window. His mother thought he looked tired, but Nadine disputes this.

"He was fine," she says. "When he got to my place he looked the same as usual. Maybe a little on the thin side, but I figured he was doing speed again, and that keeps your weight down."

The cab arrived and his mother stood at the window, watching her son walk slowly, like an old man, down the front path to where the taxi was waiting by the curb. Leo followed him out— he wanted to go for a ride. Conrad patted his brother on the head, like a puppy, and told him to go back in the house. And then he got into the cab and closed the door and the car pulled away. That was the last time Klara saw her son alive.

By the time Conrad got to his sister's place, the party was in full swing; Conrad seemed to have forgotten all about his plans to head out to the lake. Nadine remembers him making a call to Tina at one point; they were planning to go for a sauna, but afterwards Conrad hung up and continued drinking. By the time the party broke up, around 11 PM, he'd switched to tequila. Somebody gave him a lift to the Avenue Hotel, and he settled in for another hour or so of drinking.

Sometime after midnight, the owner of the hotel either drove Conrad to Vicky Ternetti's place or sent him there in a cab. Nobody's quite sure of the exact details, but what Nadine says happened next jibes with Vicky's version of the story. At 1:10 AM Klara got a call from the emergency ward of St. Joseph's

Hospital; her son was dead by the time she arrived.

"The next few days were a nightmare," Nadine says, reaching for another cigarette. "Tina was out of her mind, crying, hallucinating, she was just a complete wreck. She came here looking for drugs; Mom told her she'd found some in Conrad's old room and thrown them away. I don't think she was eating or sleeping, she was just completely out of it. Two days after my brother's funeral she called and asked to speak to him. She'd forgotten he was dead."

Tina started calling in the middle of the night, saying Conrad's friends blamed her for his death, saying they were planning to kill her. At one point she said Herbie and Bobby Cortineau had come out to the lake and run her over with her own car, left her to die.

"It was all in her head," Nadine maintains. "She was taking so many pills she was imagining things that never happened. And there were a lot of really bad types hanging out there—like that American engineer."

I've heard about this engineer before. He was in Thunder Bay that summer, working for a local diving company. He was going out with Marianne, Tina's sister, but there were rumours that he was getting it on with both of them. According to Nadine, he was pretty good-looking, and pretty nasty.

"After Tina died, people said the American had something to do with it—that she'd threatened to kill herself with the gun she had back at camp and he called her bluff. Dared her to pull the trigger. She was in with a bad crowd—she was bound to end up dead sooner or later."

Leo, who may or may not understand, nods sagely and pats his sister on the shoulder.

"Hang on a minute," Nadine says. "I want to show you something."

She leaves the room and her mother shakes her head in wonder.

"Those people," she says, referring to the crowd Tina and her son hung out with. "Scary people, I tell you. They make me frightened, all on drugs, all crazy. And Tina, she doesn't know how to go on, you know? She doesn't know how to live, with all these bad people around."

Again, Leo nods, says something I can't make out, and his mother shakes her head, sadly.

"Very bad," she says. "Very, very bad people."

Nadine returns, hands me several sheets of notepaper folded in half, then folded again.

"Tina gave this to me after Conrad died. She told me my brother wrote it and left it for her to find. It's not even his handwriting, you can tell. I think she wrote it herself, after he died."

The writing is childlike, full of spelling mistakes, and you can tell it's been written in haste, on a half-dozen pages ripped from a small, coil notebook:

> *Well my darling Im writing you this letter because there is nothing left to do. I swear I going crazy. I never write letters so dont show this anybody OK. But your an angel. This is a zoo. I really get off on you. I really think you are my best friend and I love you more than anyone before I know that. But I so fucked up.*
>
> *Help me. Help me. Help me. Help me please. I need you. Be good to me. To my mother. Stay beside me. I love you. My angel. My life. If I go come with me. Please my darling. Come with me. Come with me. I love you. Stay with me. Come with me. I wait for you.*
>
> *xxxooo Love you. Love only you. Conrad Schaeffer.*

"You might as well keep it, if you want," Nadine says. "I don't have any use for it."

Conrad's death, followed two weeks later by Tina's, killed

the party scene for a while. Several of his friends left town for Montreal to work on the boats or went to the States or South America. As for Marianne, Tina's half-sister, she went down to New Orleans and the following year she, too, was killed by a bullet to the head. She was living with the American engineer at the time.

"He could probably tell you lots about that time," Nadine says, "but you'll never find him. The last I heard he was living in Borneo, working in the oil fields."

There *is* someone I can talk to, she suggests, if I haven't already: an elderly woman named Masha who lives two doors down from Tina's old place.

"She's a bit strange," Nadine says, "a bit weird, you know what I mean? She's got this big steel fence all around her property—she's not big on visitors, that's for sure."

"Does she have a dog?" I ask.

"Masha always has a dog—Rottweilers, usually."

"Then I know her. At least, I know where she lives."

"Well, she was living out there back in the seventies, and she knew Tina. She used to take care of her dog sometimes. If you could get hold of her, she might be willing to talk to you."

Leo accompanies me to the back door and enfolds me in a powerful embrace on the doorstep. As I turn to leave, he takes hold of my arm and indicates he wants to show me something. Tossing his head forward so that a lock of dark hair falls on to his forehead, he curls his lip just so, shakes his pelvis, and snaps his fingers—Leo "Elvis" Schaeffer, the last living member of the Purple Gang.

21

A FLAT TIRE IS NATURE'S WAY OF MAKING YOU PAY
attention.

"Hang on," she says, "I see you're getting above yourself,
taking things too much for granted. Let me put this little obsta-
cle in your path, just to remind you that life isn't all fun and
games."

I'm on my way into town for my Tuesday lunch with Joan
when it happens, and my first instinct is to call her and cancel.
It's what I would have done back in Vancouver—what I would
have done a month ago, I'm sure.

But having managed out here so far—especially the two
days without power—I now feel I'm a bit of a survivalist.
Susannah Moodie I'm not, but surely I can do something as
basic as change a tire. Years ago, when Kate and Adam were
small, the tires on my old Corolla were constantly collapsing.
I'd change them by the side of the highway while the kids slept
in their car seats, generally managing to get the job done and
be back on the road before they woke up. The procedure can't
have become too much more complicated since then.

Unfortunately, changing a tire is probably a lot like dealing
with small children: you get rusty when you haven't done it for
a while. When, forty minutes later, I push open the door to the
restaurant, I'm feeling grubby but triumphant, and pleased to
see that Joan hasn't given up on me and gone home.

She lifts her glass in welcome as I approach.

"Sorry I'm late, Joan, but I have a good excuse. I got a flat
tire. And I fixed it myself."

"Good for you," she says, pouring a healthy measure of

Margie Taylor

wine into my glass. "Here's to my friend the superwoman."

"Have you been here long?"

"Actually," she says, "I came early today, but don't worry—I've been making my way through this delightful Australian Riesling and thinking about my life. It's good to see you."

Joan finishes off the rest of her glass and pours herself another. She reaches across the table, takes my hand and looks me directly in the eye.

"Alex," she says.

"Yes, Joan?"

"You know what's wrong with women?"

"What?"

"We give up too easily. We say we want it all, the big jobs, the great sex—and then the minute we turn forty, or fifty, or whatever—we give up. It's like there's some kind of cut-off point and once we pass it, we're not eligible any more. You know what I mean?"

"I'm not sure—"

"Sex," she says, emphatically. "Sex belongs to the young. That's what we believe, down deep. You're not supposed to even like sex once you're my age. You know how old I am? I'm fifty, Alex. I turned fifty on Sunday and you know what? I love sex. I do, I absolutely love it and I'm not supposed to say it. Because if there's anything worse than a dirty old man, it's a dirty old lady, right? That's really disgusting. Grab your sons and brothers, get them off the streets—there's a dirty old lady out there and she's horny for your boys."

At this point two thoughts occur to me simultaneously—Joan is absolutely pie-eyed, and her birthday was on the weekend.

"Shit, Joan. Happy birthday." And then, "Joan, are you crying?"

Because she is. At least, there are tears spilling down her cheeks, but she's also grinning and reaching for a paper napkin.

"Listen to me," she says, dabbing at her face and shaking her head. "I'm on a goddam rant. I'd say it was PMS, if I was still having my period."

"I'm so sorry, Joan. I didn't know it was your birthday, you never said—"

"Oh, hell, I don't care about my birthday."

"But you seem so upset—"

"I've been dumped." And seeing the look on my face, she starts to laugh, although fresh tears are already beginning to form in the corners of her eyes.

All I can think to say is that I didn't know she was seeing anybody.

"I know you didn't. Nobody did. Well, almost nobody."

Our waitress has come over to take our order. Joan pulls herself together and says we should have the pasta because it goes well with the Riesling, so we both order the tortellini with cream sauce. Once the waitress leaves, Joan blows her nose, takes another sip of wine and gets down to it: for the past five years, she tells me, she's been having an affair with a business-man in town. A married businessman. The owner of a local art gallery.

"We met when I was living in Montreal, and we started see-ing each other whenever he came down on business. Two or three times a year. It was just a fling, right? Something pleasant to look forward to every few months. Jimmy and I weren't get-ting along and I knew he was seeing other women, so—well, you know. And then Jimmy and I broke up and I decided to move up here. Suddenly we were seeing each other all the time. It wasn't just a fling any more; it was heavy duty. At least it was on my part. And I assumed he felt the same way."

A pause, while she blows her nose again and takes another sip of wine. She seems to have aged in the last few moments; there's a sagging of the shoulders, a weariness that wasn't there before. The crying doesn't help, of course—most of us don't look our best when our eyes are puffy and our noses are running.

David hates it when I cry. It's his British reserve, I've always thought, that makes him recoil from displays of emotion, public or private. But maybe it's just the way I look when I cry: haggard and old and bereft. Like Joan.

"God, this is boring," she says. "I feel ridiculous even talking about it. Anyway, it turns out that while he was seeing me, he was seeing somebody else. You have to admire his stamina. He's not a kid, you know; he's fifty-three. And he managed to maintain two affairs and still have occasional sex with his wife. There are men in their thirties who couldn't keep up that kind of schedule."

She's suddenly overcome by a fit of coughing—I offer her a glass of water but she waves it away with her free hand, keeping the other pressed against her mouth. Eventually she takes a deep breath and leans back against her chair.

"Sorry, that always happens when I'm upset. I've been coughing for the past two days."

"How did you find out—I mean, about the other woman?"

"She told me."

"Really?"

Joan nods and as our eyes meet, I suddenly get it.

"Oh, shit. It's Liz, isn't it? Oh, Joan, I am sorry."

She asks me if I want to hear any more, says she'll understand if I don't, Liz and me being friends and all. Which is true, Liz is my friend, but so is Joan now. And although I don't like to admit it to myself, I'm curious. I want to know what happened.

At this point the waitress returns with our orders.

"Pepper? Parmesan cheese? Anything else I can get for you ladies? No? All right then. Enjoy."

Joan looks down at her plate, takes a forkful of pasta and pushes the plate away.

"I shouldn't have ordered this, I'm not hungry."

"You should eat something," I tell her, and she grins.

"You sound like my mother. Except, come to think of it, she never said that. I don't think she ever noticed whether I was eating or not. She only noticed when I was gaining weight."

At any rate, Joan picks up her fork and pokes away at her food, while continuing with her story.

"This is a small town," she says. "You know what it's like. When I decided to move back here, Gavin—that's his name, Gavin McCormick—he said we'd have to be very careful. He knows a lot of people here. It's not like when he'd come to Montreal and we'd go to restaurants and hold hands and neck on street corners and all—"

"You necked on street corners?"

"We did lots of stupid things. I told you, he's very sexual. Anyway, he was right. I knew it was going to be different, living here. We'd have to be much more discreet. And I figured that was okay. I mean, I'm not a kid, I can behave myself in public when I have to. So mostly he came to my place and I cooked dinners for him, and we rented porn videos and had a lot of sex."

"Did you rent the porn videos or did he?"

"We both did. You know, if you want me to get through this without another coughing fit you're going to have to button up."

"Sorry. Go on."

For the first year or so, she says, things were fine. They got away a few times, took a trip to Barbados, went to Vegas a couple of times. Now and then they drove across the border and spent a weekend in Minneapolis. Joan was crazy about him—he was the first man she'd met in years who didn't bore her. I'm dying to know how they managed all these little holidays when Gavin was still living with his wife, but I don't dare interrupt.

"Anyway." She takes another sip of her drink and stares into the glass, fondling the stem with her thumb and index finger. "I guess I was starting to find it difficult, keeping him to myself, you know? I mean, keeping the *fact* of him to myself, not telling anybody. He was so good-looking, and I was just so crazy about him—I really wanted to confide in someone. And it was hard keeping it from Liz. For one thing, she knows me so well, and every now and then she'd try to hook me up with somebody. And of course, I wasn't interested in meeting anybody else. Why would I be? I had the perfect man."

"Who was married to somebody else." I know I'm interrupting but I can't help it.

"Who was married to somebody else," she repeats. "And that was fine with me. I told you, I'm not interested in getting married again. I tried it twice and that's enough for anybody. Unless you're Liza Minelli. And besides, I was still married myself. So I couldn't have married Gavin even if I'd wanted to."

"I thought you and Jimmy were divorced. Honestly, Joan, you are just full of surprises today."

She smiles. "I left Jimmy, but I never divorced him. I think I felt that as long as I was still legally married to the guy, I couldn't fall into the trap of marrying somebody else. And he seemed to feel the same way. At least, he's never sued for divorce. I think we're both pretty happy to just let things carry on the way they are."

"So what happened next, with you and this Gavin person?"

"Well, about eighteen months ago, Liz decided to have a

dinner party. She wanted to show off her dining suite—you know, the oak table and chairs and the hutch that goes with it? She'd got it the year before but she'd only just finished paying for it. So it was kind of a celebration, I guess. And I decided to bring Gavin. He wasn't hot on the idea, but I explained there were only going to be eight of us, and I named everybody and he didn't know any of them, so he finally agreed. I made kind of a thing about it, I guess. I'd just had it with all this sneaking around and I wanted to show people I wasn't this lonely, dried-up old spinster. I wanted to show them I had a man."

And show them she did. Gavin was charming and the women all drooled over him and the men liked him because he's a man's man—as Joan says, "Believe me, you can't *not* like Gavin McCormick." The only one who held back a little at first was Liz. Joan had told her about him ahead of time, told her he was married and they'd been seeing each other for a few years. Joan could tell Liz didn't approve. By the end of the night, though, Gavin had won her over, and the next morning she called Joan to positively gush over him.

"She told me she was so thrilled for me, so happy that I had someone like Gavin in my life. I mean, really, she got quite tearful about it."

"Was she faking it, do you think?"

"No, I don't think so. I think she really meant it. And it was a relief, you know? To have someone to talk to about him, someone who'd met him and liked him. Someone who wouldn't judge."

And so over the next few months, Joan and her lover began having regular nights at Liz's house, intimate little dinner parties where often it was just the three of them, and Gavin would share his attentions equally between the two women. Joan was delighted that her man and her best friend enjoyed each other's

Margie Taylor

company; she even encouraged them to get to know each other independently. If the phone rang when Gavin was over, and it was Liz, she'd often put him on the phone while she checked out the meal in the oven. She would come back to the living room to find him engaged in an animated discussion about art, or some other aspect of high culture. Because Liz, to Joan's surprise and admiration, had recently taken up painting.

Gavin was very supportive. While not a fan, for the most part, of amateur art, he told Joan it was brave and daring of her friend to explore her creative instincts, as he put it. After dinner at Liz's one night, she reluctantly brought out a few of her paintings to show them, and Gavin announced that, in his opinion, Liz had a gift, there was something remarkable and insightful in her brush strokes and if she went on like this, he might be tempted at some time to mount a show of her works in his gallery.

"You should have seen Lizzie's face," Joan said. "It was like she'd just been given the keys to heaven. She sat there watching him, concentrating on his every word, and I really thought she was going to burst into tears. And it was weird, because to tell you the truth, I didn't think her paintings were all that good."

"So you think he was lying?"

Again, the shrug. "Who knows? Maybe they were something special, what do I know? What about you—have you seen them?"

I shake my head. "No, I never have. She told me she was painting a couple of years ago but she hasn't mentioned it in ages. I got the impression she wasn't doing it any more."

Joan says, "I think you're right. I think she got to the point where she knew she wasn't going to be a first-class painter, and Liz doesn't ever like to be mediocre. She likes to be the best. But for a while there, Gavin was stopping by her place two or three days a week, to check on how she was doing. I'd see him on the weekend and he'd tell me all about it, how Liz was really coming along, how she'd done this portrait of her mother and it was really special, really revealing. He talked about her all the time."

None of this bothered Joan in the slightest. She was seeing her lover as much as she always had, he was as attentive as he'd always been, and they were still taking their trips down to the States from time to time. And, she adds, he was sleeping with her, not Liz.

"You're sure about that?"

She nods. "Absolutely. Back then, when he was spending all this time acting as her mentor and telling me about it, I just know they weren't going to bed together. I would have picked up on it if they had been. He was just too open about it all—if I asked him he could have accounted for every minute."

"So what happened?"

What happened was that Gavin stopped talking about Liz. He stopped dropping in on her, stopped telling Joan about her painting, and Liz stopped inviting them for dinner.

"All of a sudden," Joan says, "the two of them acted like they'd gone off each other."

"Hmm."

"Yes. 'Hmm.' I should have known, I guess, I should have figured something was up. I'd call her and see if she wanted us to drop by, and she'd be busy. Or I'd say something to him like, 'Why don't we have dinner with Liz this weekend?', and he'd say we saw too much of her. And so finally I just thought, well, they've had an argument, maybe he criticized her paintings— you know how sensitive Liz can be. And so I just left it alone. I mean, it was nice having them like each other, but it was also nice having him all to myself again, I have to admit."

And according to Joan, for the next year or so, life contin-ued pretty much as normal. She saw Gavin two or three times a week, they went on their little trips, and although she didn't see much of Liz, she assumed her friend was wrapped up in one of her never-ending projects, and too busy to socialize.

And then, two days ago, Liz dropped her bombshell.

"It was my birthday," Joan says, "and Gavin was coming over for dinner. I'd made a cake—chocolate rum gateau, absolutely deadly. And I knew he'd give me something nice, he always makes a big deal out of birthdays."

She smiles briefly, remembering, then asks me if she's bor-ing me to tears. "It really is such a cliché, isn't it, this kind of stuff? I hate women who let themselves be victims and then moan about it. You can tell me to shut up, I won't be offended."

"Go on."

"Well, I'm sitting there, and it's getting later and later, and I suddenly get this really bad feeling in the pit of my stomach. I know he's not coming. And the minute I realize that, the phone rings and it's Liz and she sounds like she's been crying. At first I can't get what she's saying, she's all muffled up and kind of whispering, and then I realize she's telling me how bad she feels, how sorry she is, she never meant to hurt me, neither of them did, it just happened, they didn't mean it to happen—on and on and on. She says it was kismet, the two of them are kindred spirits, their minds meet on some elevated, transcendent plane. She wants me to know that it isn't just sex, it's more of an intellectual relationship. He's teaching her so much, he's reading to her, helping her to broaden her mind. And when she finally pauses for breath, I ask her if Gavin is there, with her, and she says, 'Yes, he is,' and she asks if I want to speak to him and I say, 'Tell him to go fuck him-self,' and I hang up the phone."

displaced PERSONS

"Oh, Joan, I'm so sorry."

"I went into the kitchen, threw the cake in the garbage and poured myself a Scotch."

The waitress has been hovering for the past five minutes, waiting for an appropriate moment to bring us our bill. I guess she decides it's now or never because she comes to our table, plunks the bill down on the table, swoops up our empty glasses and smiles.

"If you ladies wouldn't mind settling up, that would be great. I go off work in ten minutes."

"Let me get this." I reach for the bill and although Joan puts up a fight, you can tell her heart isn't in it. "My treat for your birthday." Her eyes fill with tears, and I immediately regret saying that. "I'm sorry, Joan—I shouldn't have mentioned your birthday. That was stupid of me."

She shakes her head, reaches for another tissue from the napkin dispenser and blows her nose, vigorously. "It isn't that," she says. "I was just remembering this bumper sticker I saw a few years ago: 'My husband ran off with my best friend—and I really miss her!'"

Joan looks up at me, and in spite of her puffy eyes, her red nose, and the tiny cracks and fissures around her mouth, she looks like a lost child. I'm tempted to take her in my arms and give her a hug right there and then. I would, if it wasn't for the waitress standing inches away, patently wanting us to pay our bill so she can get out of there and go home.

"I miss my friend," Joan tells me, and I nod.

"Of course you do. I'll bet she misses you, too."

As Joan stands up and struggles on with her coat, she tells me she thinks our relationship has turned a corner.

"They say if you can cry in front of someone, you must really trust them. I think we're becoming good friends, don't you?"

Margie Taylor

    And then I do give her that hug, in spite of the waitress. We
toddle out of the restaurant together, two girlfriends who've had
a bit too much to drink, but have remembered to leave a hefty
tip. We'll be back, after all, next Tuesday.

22

"ARE YOU STILL SPEAKING TO ME?"

It's been two days since Joan told me about Gavin, and I've been expecting this call ever since. I knew Liz would feel nervous, a little defensive, perhaps, and I would try hard not to sound judgmental. It would not be a particularly easy conversation.

"Don't be silly. How are you?"

"Fine." She doesn't sound particularly fine, to my ears. "I was afraid you'd disown me or something."

"We're all grown-ups, aren't we?"

"Are we? I feel pretty un-grown-up at the moment."

For one moment I think she's about to cry, and I wonder if something's gone wrong with her and Gavin. Maybe she's regretting the choice she made.

"What I *would* like to know," I say, "is why you didn't tell me yourself? I mean, you've been seeing this guy for over a year, and I've been here since September. Why didn't you say something?"

"I was going to. I'd planned on telling you about him when you came out—I thought we'd go for dinner somewhere and have a nice talk and I would just tell you, you know? I mean, this isn't the kind of thing you like to get into over the phone."

I can understand that, it makes sense. Most of the important things that have happened in my life have been discussed over dinners in small Italian restaurants, with lots of red wine to get the verbal juices flowing.

"So why didn't you?"

"Because—" And now she sounds exasperated, she sounds

Margie Taylor

like the Liz I know well, who sees her plans, carefully laid, foiled because of the carelessness or stupidity of others. "I was waiting for the right time—I didn't want to just plunge into it. And the next thing I knew, you started hanging out with Joan, and I was afraid you'd tell her. Or you'd be pissed off with me telling you and then expecting you to keep it a secret. What with you and her having lunch all the time."

I have to admit, that would have been difficult. "I guess you're right—I probably wouldn't have wanted to know about it, if it meant keeping it secret from her."

"Exactly. And you can't lie worth a damn, it shows all over your face. I figured if she guessed and asked you about Gavin and me, you wouldn't be able to lie to her. I didn't want to put you in that position."

"But in the end you told her yourself—you were able to keep it from her all that time, why'd you go and tell her now? And on her birthday, Liz. I mean, to be honest, it sounds a little cruel."

I can't help it; determined as I am not to be critical, or at least not to sound it, that note of censure creeps in. And Liz can hear it. There's silence on the other end of the line. I wonder if she's going to hang up on me. Eventually, she just says, "It wasn't my call."

"What do you mean? She told me you phoned her."

She sighs. "No, I mean it wasn't my decision. I wanted him to keep that date. I knew it was her birthday, I knew it was important to her. But he didn't want to. In fact, he refused. He came to my place and said he wasn't doing this any more, he said he loved me and wanted to be with me. It was him or Joan, he said. I couldn't have both."

"But—" This isn't making any sense. The man is *married*, for heaven's sake. Who's he to go around laying down ultima-

tums? As calmly as possible, given the absurdity of the situation, I put this to Liz, who pauses once again—she's fond of
the dramatic pause—and then says, "He's leaving his wife,
Alex. He's left her. For me."

"You're kidding."

I don't know why—I don't even know this Gavin person—
but I am completely taken aback by this. Here's a man in his
fifties, a playboy, obviously, who blithely carries on affairs with
two women for over a year, and suddenly decides on the spur of
the moment to leave his wife for one of them. It's the kind of
thing that almost never happens—no, it never happens. Liz is
either lying or deluded.

"I'm not kidding," she says. "He moved out last Friday
night. He's been staying with me ever since, and this morning
he went to see his lawyer. He's getting a divorce."

"Jesus."

"Yes," she agrees. "It's kind of amazing, isn't it?"

"I don't know what to say. Do you love him?"

"Well, of course I love him. What kind of a person do you
think I am? Do you think I'd go out and steal a man away from
his wife *and* his girlfriend just for the heck of it? Honestly, Alex,
I would've thought you knew me better than that."

Now I really don't know what to say. We've had arguments
in the past, Liz and I, misunderstandings, really; we usually
manage to sort them out before too much damage is done. At
the moment, I'm beginning to resent the fact that I've been
drawn into this at all. It's not as though I live here anymore. It
really has nothing to do with me, yet here I am in the middle
of it. And then she says—and her voice is pregnant with meaning—"I would have thought *you'd* understand, Alex. You of all
people."

My first thought is that Joan has given away my secret. I

can't believe it of her, I thought she'd be more discreet. Before I can say anything, Liz says, "As I recall, David was still married when you met him."

Relieved, I explain that David didn't leave his wife for me, although he may have wanted to.

"We didn't start seeing each other until after he and Jane split up. He called me later."

"Four days later," she says.

"Look, Liz—"

I stop myself and take a deep breath. If we carry on much longer like this, one of us is going to get angry and slam the phone down. And if that happens, it'll take some time to patch things up. Neither of us is good at fixing these kind of things. I make up my mind to take the high road.

"Liz, I don't think either of us wants to be having this conversation. Why don't we get together for dinner, sit down like you said over a bottle of wine and have a good talk, okay? It's been ages."

She seizes on this as a reprieve. We agree to meet Saturday night, at a small Italian place in the north end of town that's been open for just a few months.

"Gavin and I go there all the time," she tells me, happy now, restored to her usual self. "They make the best gnocchi. You like gnocchi, don't you? I remember you used to order it all the time. You'll just love this place."

⌘ ⌘ ⌘

Ten minutes later the phone rings—again; I pick it up feeling very Dorothy Parker-ish: What fresh hell is this?

It's David, and he wants to know if I sent the letter.

"No. I didn't even write it. I'm sorry, David. I did try."

There's a pause. I'm about to attempt to explain when he says, "I've been thinking about what you said, and I've decided to come back early. The work's not going as well as I'd hoped—I think I need a break. I'm heading back to Vancouver in a week and I think you should, too."

"Now, just a minute, David—"

"Don't get your knickers in a twist," he says. "I didn't mean it like that. I'm not trying to order you around. What I mean is—Christ, I don't know what the hell I mean."

Trying to stay calm, I tell him he can't just reorganize things like this. If he wants to reshuffle his own agenda, fine, but I'm not letting him do it for me. I have my own plans, I've rented this place till Christmas, and I may keep it for longer. It's just so damned *David* of him to think that because *he's* changed his plans, I'll just shelve all my own work, pack up the dog, and the computer and head home, like a good little wife. The man doesn't have a clue about the person he married. It's a good thing we're not having this conversation in person, because if we were, I swear I'd strangle him.

"I'm sorry," he tells me, when I eventually run out of things to say. "I think I'm homesick."

The statement takes me off guard. For a moment I forget to be furious.

"Homesick for what?"

"For Canada, I guess."

He says he wants to see snow and frost on the window-panes and kids in tuques and mittens. He wants to see clear blue winter skies and frozen lakes. He wants to be warm and comfortable indoors and know it's minus twenty outside.

"Then you should come here. You're homesick for northern Ontario, not Vancouver. Vancouver's just like England at Christmas, only with mountains."

Margie Taylor

"But the mountains are snow-capped," he argues, "and the children go ice-skating. And people are hearty and cheerful and they drink rum toddies and wish each other good cheer."

"You're describing a painting by Kurelek. Christmas in Vancouver is wet and grey and sloppy—it doesn't even deserve to be called Christmas."

"All right," he says. "You're right. It's not just that, it's more than that. It's us. I feel like I should come back so we can talk."

"I don't want to spend Christmas talking, David. I don't think it will help."

"What will help?" he says. "Go on, Alex, tell me. What do you want?"

What I want is to find my way back into the past and stay there. I want my children back as babies; I want hours spent chasing after toddlers and picnics at the beach, birthday parties with a dozen raucous youngsters ripping up the house and a kitchen full of moms drinking cheap champagne and taking it in turns to venture out into the living room to try to instill some order. And then, failing utterly, returning to the kitchen to inform the group that nobody appears to be bleeding and are there any of those marvelous little pizza things left?

I want the hugs my son used to give me two or three times a day, huge bear hugs that almost knocked me over, charging towards me to grab me around the knees, just checking in to make sure I was there. I want to walk home from school hand-in-hand with my daughter, while she talks non-stop about what everybody said and how they said it and what she thinks will happen tomorrow. I want to stop from time to time, as I did in those days, and concentrate on the moment—the colour of the sky, the way the wind feels in my face, the aura surrounding my daughter's hair in the sunlight—and know that this moment is important because it is unique: I won't get it back.

Even then, though, even in those moments of awareness, I thought the story would continue. I didn't really believe, surrounded by children and family and so much responsibility, that I would ever be alone again. It didn't seem possible.

David is waiting five thousand miles away, in a small, square room on a university campus, waiting for an answer. I take a deep breath, and begin:

"David, last year I had an affair."

23

EVERYTHING THAT HAPPENS IN THIS TOWN HAPPENS over lunch or dinner. Liz has brought Gavin along, like a cat showing off her prey. He's seated with his back to me. When I enter the restaurant, he turns around in response to Liz's wave and watches me critically, I think, but not unkindly. With interest. A man who's spent a lifetime appraising women and gauging his effect upon them. I'm prepared not to like him.

His presence here is a surprise to me, but not a disappointment. At least now I'll get a chance to see what all the fuss is about. His being here will have an effect on our conversation, certainly, but that's not necessarily a bad thing. Women behave better when men are around. We're inclined to be bitchy when we're on our own, which is what makes getting together with "the girls" both fun and a strain.

Liz is immediately apologetic but not remorseful. "I hope you don't mind," she tells me, trying not to appear smug. "I know you weren't expecting Gavin to be here. But at the last minute I made him come with me. I wanted him to meet you—I want you to know each other."

If Gavin resents being brought out and put on display like this, he doesn't show it. He takes my hand in a warm, affectionate grip and smiles broadly while his glistening hazel eyes, magnified by a pair of wire-rimmed glasses, seek out my own with an intensity that is surely practiced and meant to be flattering. Which it is. He reminds me of someone, someone I'm sure I used to know very well. For the life of me, the name escapes me.

"Alex. It's good to meet you. Finally," he adds, as if not

meeting me was the one thing preventing him from truly enjoying life for the past few years. "Liz and Joan are quite crazy about you, you know that?"

Now this does take me aback, just a little. I hadn't expected Joan's name to be mentioned. And I see that this, too, is deliberate: he wants to unsettle me, he wants to throw me off the scent. You're good, I think, smiling back into that handsome, rather boyish face. You're very good, Mr. McCormick.

Once the introductions are completed, there's a moment of awkwardness as we decide where I should sit. Gavin settles the matter by gently pulling me down next to him, so that I can sit facing Liz and give him a chance to get to know me, as he puts it. I'd prefer to be on the other side; with inches between us, I'm only too aware of the clean, soapy scent of the man, with maybe just a hint of something alcoholic. Liz tells me they arrived early—they're halfway through a bottle of wine, and she says she'd better order something to eat soon.

"Drinking on an empty stomach, I'll be pissed to the gills in about fifteen minutes," she says and laughs, exchanging glances with Gavin over her menu.

"We wouldn't want that, now, would we?" he responds, with a smile in my direction. Then, leaning towards me, he confides in a fake stage whisper that my friend Liz is terrible when she's drunk, so we'd better do our best to keep her sober. I find myself instinctively drawing back; I hate this kind of assumed intimacy, on such short notice. It's almost always faked. This is no doubt exactly what he did that night at Liz's party, when Joan brought him for the first time to meet her friends. I can picture him working his wiles on Liz, little by little charming the pants off her, until he did, eventually, remove them.

Well, forget it, mister, this broad's made of sterner stuff. I've been immunized against men like you. You won't get anywhere with me. And after my experience with Dr. Jim, even the fact that you smell terrific will get you nowhere. Absolutely nowhere.

When the waiter comes by to take our orders, Gavin suggests I might want to try the gnocchi; they make it the old-fashioned way, and Liz has told him what a fan I am of the dish. Perversely, I order the veal instead—partly to show him I have a mind of my own and partly to shock Liz, who takes the veal situation very seriously and refuses to eat it because of the way the animals are treated during their brief lifetimes. I've argued before that if she's really going to put her money where her mouth is, she should become a vegetarian, as chickens live their lives penned together in the dark; pigs are transported miles in rotten conditions before they're slaughtered, and if you think a fish feels nothing as it slaps around in a boat gasping its life out for minutes on end, you are seriously deluded. She doesn't care about these creatures; only the plight of the veal calf captures her sympathy.

So there I sit, determined to horrify my good friend and dislike her boyfriend. The latter, I'm finding, is difficult. There is no doubt that the man is everything Liz and Joan said he was: intelligent, attractive, and good-humoured. It's too early to tell whether or not he's actually witty but you can see he's definitely what my father would have called "well-spoken." He volunteers very little about himself, asking instead about me, which is an attractive quality in anyone, especially a man. My writing, my family—on the surface, at least, Gavin is intensely interested in all of this, and a good deal of the time spent waiting for our order to arrive is taken up with my account of the progress I've made with my novel and the state of things with David, Kate, and Adam. It's not a surprise that he knows their names already, courtesy of Joan and Liz, but the fact that he has remembered

them goes a long way towards making inroads in my estima-
tion. I have longtime girlfriends, for heaven's sake, who forget
my children's names from time to time.

In turn, he tells me about his own children, a teenage son
and daughter, a few years younger than mine. A funny story
about his youngest, the boy, a telling incident concerning his
daughter. He's drawing me in; sensing my own joy in Kate and
Adam, he's showing me that he, too, loves his kids.

Liz doesn't say much, she seems content to take a back seat
and let the two of us get to know each other. From time to time,
I catch her gazing at him with a look that is somewhere
between lust and maternal pride. Gavin sees this and teases
her: "Did I get an 'A' on my report card, Mom?"

"Oh, shut up." She turns to me with a laugh. "He's a bug-
ger, isn't he? He won't let me get away with anything."

At this point the waiter reappears; together, he and Gavin
discuss the wine list. Gavin favours the 1995 Brunello di
Montalcino, the most expensive bottle on the list. When Liz and
I balk at the price, he insists it's to be his treat. So chalk up two
more points for Gavin: he likes his wine and he's not averse to
spending his money. The first bottle he ordered was a Chianti
and while I'm strictly plebeian when it comes to the grape, I
have to admit it went down a treat, as David's mother would say.

When the waiter comes with the veal, I regret my impulse
immediately. When Gavin's gnocchi is laid before him, it's
smothering, luscious comfort food—delectable potato
dumplings in a sauce that smells delicious. I hate veal and this
particular piece is a little underdone, which will no doubt make
me gag midway through the first bite. Reading my mind, Gavin
says not a word but picks up our plates and exchanges them.
Then he hands me my fork and says simply, "Eat." It's avuncular and probably a little patronizing, and I should react with

indignation and chagrin. Instead I give him a foolish little smile, say thanks, and dig into the best gnocchi I've had.

We are well into our main course before Joan's name is brought up again; this time it's Liz who wants to know how she's doing. Cautiously—because these kinds of conversations can be minefields—I reply that I think she's doing pretty well, considering.

"Considering." Liz repeats the word thoughtfully, chewing it over like an unexpected piece of gristle in her steak.

"Well, you know. I mean, it was a shock; she really wasn't expecting it."

"No, I guess she wasn't." Liz puts down her fork and gazes out into the dimness of the room. For a moment I'm afraid she's going to cry. If my friends are all going to start sobbing over their food, I'm going to have to give up eating out altogether.

"She's doing terrific, actually." Gavin pauses and clears his throat. "I went to see her this afternoon, and we had a very good talk. Personally, I think she's going to come out of this just fine."

"You've seen her?" Liz is looking at him in horror, as if he's just admitted to something particularly loathsome. "Gavin, you didn't. How could you? Why would you do that?"

Unperturbed, he reaches for the wine bottle and tops up our glasses, all three of them. While doing so, he explains, in a calm, reasonable tone, that Joan and he were lovers for more than five years, that he still considers her a friend, and he's spent the past week worrying about her. So today he decided to call her up and see if she'd let him drop by.

"I wouldn't have blamed her if she'd hung up the phone on me," he says. "But she didn't. She was a little cold, which is understandable, but in the end she said I could come over and have coffee. Cheers."

The three of us raise our glasses and click them together,

but Gavin's the only one who drinks. Liz and I are still discombobulated by this turn of events. Almost in unison, we demand to know, "What happened?"

"Well, I told her I was having dinner with the two of you tonight." He turns to me and says, "She told me I'd like you and she gave me absolute permission to flirt with you at will. She says your husband has run off to England. Is that correct?"

"He's on sabbatical." And then, for some reason, I feel the need to add, "He'll be back at Christmas."

"Aha. I see."

Now Liz cuts in, demanding to know what, for God's sake, did Joan have to say about her?

"Not much," he says, which disappoints her. "She's going back east."

"Moving? She's moving back to Montreal?" Liz sounds both surprised and offended.

"Toronto," he says. "She's decided to make a fresh start."

"I don't believe it."

Gavin shrugs and returns to his veal scaloppini. You can believe it or not, he says, but she's putting the house up for sale in January. She'll move as soon as it's sold. Hearing him say this, I can see now that it makes perfect sense: she came here for him, why would she stay?

"Good for her," I say, and Liz turns on me as if I'd personally attacked her.

"Why would you say that?" Which she amends to, "*How* could you say that? Honestly, Alex, I thought you were my friend."

A little smugly, I reply that this isn't about her, it's about Joan. And if Joan wants to leave town, why shouldn't she?

"Because she's abandoning me. She's turning tail and running away right when I need her most."

"What on earth," I want to know, "could you possibly need from Joan at the moment? I mean—" and here I indicate Gavin sitting to my right—"I thought you had everything you needed."

The jibe is lost on Liz. Her pale blue eyes fill with tears and she gazes forlornly back and forth between Gavin and myself, like a lost child. Sheep, actually, I correct myself. Right now my good friend Liz looks like nothing so much as a great sad-eyed sheep. Like the one Alice encountered in *Through the Looking-Glass*, the one with the knitting needles who ran the shop that turned into a boat floating downstream.

"It's not fair," she bleats. "Everybody I love is leaving me."

This is Gavin's cue to speak up and reassure her that *he* is not leaving, my darling—*he* will stay tried and true. Instead he grins at me and reaches over and pats her hand.

"Eat your steak, sweetheart," he tells her. "Your dinner's getting cold. And let's get the waiter over here—time for another bottle of wine, I think."

But Liz is determined not to be cheered up so easily. She wants to wallow just a little longer. "But Gavin, what will I do? I've known Joan for years, almost as long as Alex. I got to know her right after Bruno and I broke up. She and I went to Divorcees Anonymous together, and we took a class together at the college. Conversational Spanish—I can still remember it: *Esta un gorilla en casa? Es ridiculo, no es un gorilla en casa.* Oh, shit."

And now she is crying, big watery sheep tears streaming down that pale, pretty face, and all Gavin and I can do is repeat the phrase to each other, which suddenly seems hysterically funny.

"Oh, Liz, I'm sorry," I tell her, not looking sorry at all, "I know you're upset, but honestly—why would they teach you something like that?"

"I don't know, I guess they thought it would come in handy. If you were ever in Mexico."

Gavin wants to know what else she remembers from the course, and Liz dries her eyes and thinks for a moment and then comes out with, "*Donde esta mi abrigo? No se, lo siento mucho.*"

"What's *abrigo*?" he asks.

"Overcoat," she says. "*Where is my overcoat? I don't know. Sorry.*"

"Was this, I don't know, tied in somehow to the gorilla experience?" Gavin asks. "I mean, did your teacher think it was possible that in Mexico gorillas came into houses and stole people's overcoats? Was that the idea?"

"Oh, shut up."

But she's out of her soppy, sorry-for-herself mood and back to tackling her steak. Gavin empties the rest of that bottle into our glasses and orders another. When the waiter returns he presents the bottle to Gavin and positively salivates over him; waiters love people who order lots of booze. For one thing, you tend to eat more if you're drinking, and the tip you leave is higher.

Although I'm not against another glass of wine, I remind Gavin that he said earlier we have to keep Liz sober: "You're doing a lousy job of it, if you don't mind my saying."

"You know, you're absolutely right. Elizabeth, you are not to drink out of this bottle, is that understood? Alex and I will share this between us and you will have coffee and sober the hell up."

"Screw you," she says fondly, and he shakes his head at me.

"What'd I tell you? She's a nasty drunk."

And that's when it comes to me.

"Malcolm McDowell."

"I beg your pardon?"

"That's who you remind me of—Malcolm McDowell in *A Clockwork Orange.* You look exactly like him."

Margie Taylor

"And is that a good thing?"

"Yes, it is, as a matter of fact. I always thought he was extremely sexy."

"Then I'm flattered." He raises his glass in the air and proposes a toast, "To Malcolm McDowell and all who sail him."

Liz and I both raise our glasses—"To Malcolm"—and drink. I feel intensely warm and comfortable, part of a tight little circle of goodwill, accepted and accepting. We could live together, the three of us, settle down in this town and make our homes together and live happily ever after. Little tongues of sexual anticipation are working their way down my spine; wine is the most potent aphrodisiac I know. Four to five glasses and I could take on the fifth fleet; seven or eight and I want only to curl up and wake up safely, in my own bed.

Liz is smiling at me—good old, familiar Liz, her youthful vitality in evidence despite the wrinkling at the eyes and in the corners of her wide, lusty mouth. Liz, I think, I could take you in my arms right here in this restaurant, shock the whole damn place with a thrust of my tongue down your throat.

Gavin speaks, and his voice comes from somewhere far away. His hand, warm and slightly damp, has somehow come to rest on my upper thigh. I turn to him, ask him to repeat it.

"Do you want dessert?" he says, removing his hand and reaching to take the menu from the waiter, who has materialized to my left. (It was asexual, that touch, he just wanted to get my attention. But it has been so long since a man touched me anywhere; the imprint of his hand stays on my skin.)

"I'll just have coffee," I tell him, and Liz agrees. "With something in it, maybe," she adds. "Whisky or Kahlúa or something."

We order three Irish coffees and once the waiter has departed, I shift myself, just a little, so that my right knee is pressing, lightly, against Gavin's. It seems to me he tenses slightly, but his knee stays put. Taking this as an invitation, or at least not an outright rejection, I slowly move my right foot until it is linked around his left, and place my hand just above his knee. For the next few minutes, while we wait for the waiter to bring our drinks, I allow my fingers to knead the soft, pliant fabric of his suit, enjoying the firm, hard muscle beneath my touch.

Liz is telling a funny story about a woman at work. With the finesse of a geisha, I keep up with the tale, interjecting at all the appropriate moments, while slowly working my way up his thigh towards his crotch. Gavin has fallen silent; it may be my imagination but his breathing sounds laboured to my ear. My fingers arrive at their destination; what I'm not imagining is the swelling here, and the heat emanating from his body. I have not felt this kind of power in years. I love it.

Eventually, the waiter appears with our coffee and with a final, gentle squeeze I remove my hand and bring it up to the table, out of harm's way. Gavin clears his throat and says something about needing a glass of water.

"Are you okay?" Liz asks, and hands him her water, untouched.

"I'm fine," he tells her. "It's just a little hot in here."

She gazes at him fondly, then turns back to me. "He's so good-looking, don't you think? Come on, Alex, admit it, don't you think he's gorgeous?"

Turning to look directly at him for the first time since assaulting him, I stare into his handsome face—grave and unsmiling at the moment—and announce that he's gorgeous. "I could go to bed with Gavin in a minute."

Liz is triumphant. "You see, Gavin? I was right. I knew she'd like you. You're what the kids call a babe magnet."

This does it. Gavin picks up his napkin and throws it across the table at her. "For Chrissake, Lizzie, you're pissed. Both of you. I hate to say it but you're a couple of cheap drunks."

But you can hear in his voice that he's amused in spite of himself, and maybe a little flattered. Lifting his glass to both of us, he adds, "To the dames. There is nothin' like a dame!"

"*Guys and Dolls*?" I ask.

He corrects me: "*South Pacific*, actually."

I tell him I never saw it and he says he doesn't believe me. "That's like saying you never saw *The Sound of Music*."

"Well, actually—"

"Stop!" He holds up his hand in mock protest. "Enough. I refuse to believe it. Everyone on earth has seen *The Sound of Music* at least five times."

"Not me," I tell him.

"How did you miss it?"

"I think I was reading a book."

"Ah. An intellectual," he says, and I hasten to correct that impression.

"Not completely. I loved *Beach Blanket Bingo*."

"Oh, me too," says Liz. "Didn't you always want to be Annette? She was just so perfect. *How to Stuff a Wild Bikini*— that was my all-time favourite. Did you see it?"

I saw them all, but by the end, I tell her, they were getting a tad derivative.

"She has MS, you know," Liz says, and I nod.

"I know. My mother had it too."

"Oh, God, Alex, I forgot." Liz reaches over and grabs my hand in hers and gives it a comforting squeeze. "You poor kid."

"Yeah." I'm close to tears—we both are—and Gavin decides it's time to bring the party to an end.

"Down the hatch, ladies," he says. "Let's end the night on a cheerful note."

Liz takes a sip of her coffee and wipes a creamy shaving from her lip. Leaning across the table, she confides in me that Gavin, she fears, is a bit of snob when it comes to the movies.

"He likes art house films," she says. "You know—subtitles and documentaries and everything dark and raining all the time. The kind of stuff that makes you want to go home and open a vein."

Gavin turns to me and smiles. "I'm working on expanding her horizons, but as you can see I'm not getting very far."

So, we're conspirators again. The feel-up under the table is forgiven, if not forgotten. As if to confirm what Gavin has just said, Liz announces that *Cannonball Run* was highly underrated. He shakes his head in despair.

"I give up, my little sugarplum. When it comes to the movies, you're a peon."

It's all an act; I know that and I'm sure Gavin does, as well. Liz and I've been friends for thirty years and we both know she's more sophisticated than she's letting on. These, then, are the roles they've adopted—peasant and professor, simple village girl and highfalutin' art critic. I'm tempted to call her on it, but only because I'm a little jealous: they're obviously enjoying each other and if it spices things up a little, what harm does it do? It could get tedious if one was around them for great lengths of time, but as I'm off to Vancouver next month I'll take the magnanimous route. Raising my glass, I declare that it's my turn to make a toast.

"To friends. Old and new." And, with a grin that threatens once again to become tearful, I add, "I love you guys."

And right at that moment I do.

24

MY DINNER WITH LIZ AND GAVIN HAS LEFT A NASTY taste in my mouth. Which is probably the result of the booze I drank—at least an entire bottle of wine to myself, not to mention the Irish coffee. Gavin was the only one to leave completely on his own two feet; both Liz and I had to be helped out of the place, which would have embarrassed me at any other time but for the fact that we were the last people left in the restaurant, so only the waiter and the owner of the place were on hand to bear witness.

I remember a taxi pulling up to the front door of the restaurant, Gavin helping me into the back seat—ohmigod, did I feel him up again? I have a vague recollection of reaching under his jacket as he struggled to fasten my seat belt. And I kissed him, I remember that. I aimed for his mouth, but I think at the last minute he turned and brushed his cheek against my lips.

God. How embarrassing. The feel-up under the table reconstructs itself as I lie in bed, remembering: What on earth was I thinking of? I was drunk, obviously, but how—goofy, that's the only word for it. What must he think of me?

Ten minutes later, as I am struggling to find the will to get up and see to the dog, the telephone rings. It's Gavin, calling to see how I'm doing and if I want him to bring my car out to the lake. I am confused.

"I'm sorry, I don't understand. What about my car? You want to take it for a drive?"

And so he patiently explains that we agreed to leave my car in the restaurant parking lot, after receiving the assurances of the owner that no harm would come to it. "None of us were in any shape to drive. I called a cab for Liz and me, too."

I don't remember paying for the cab; he says he had the driver put it on his tab. It must have cost him a fortune. The drive out to the lake is a good forty minutes and I'm willing to bet the cabbie had to drive around a bit before finding this place. I can't imagine I was much help with directions.

"Gavin, I'll pay you back—"

"Don't be silly. I just wanted to make sure you were all right. How are you feeling?"

"Fine," I tell him, lying through my teeth. "I was just going to head out for a walk."

"Great," he says. "Best thing for a hangover." He goes on to say he held on to my keys last night and is now proposing to head down to the restaurant, pick up my car and drive it out to the lake.

"Oh, surely that won't be necessary. I don't want you driving all the way out here—it's too far."

It's bad enough making chitchat with the guy, after what happened last night; I certainly don't want to have to meet him in the flesh for the next, say, seventeen years or so.

But Gavin is persistent. Eventually we agree that he will drive out in the early afternoon to give me the car. And I, in turn, will drive him back to town afterwards. We will be spending, at the very least, a good hour and a half in each other's company. Looking for an out, I suggest it would be just as easy for me to get a cab into the city, but he says he's curious to see the lake at this time of year. Maybe he'll bring Liz; a little fresh air might help brush away the fog.

It's not much comfort knowing Liz is as hungover as me. I'm old enough to know better—we both are. One of the few compensations of maturity should be an understanding of one's limits. I should be past the point of saying to hell with it, tonight I'm going to have a good time. Which is what I've done too often in my life. The "I deserve it" mentality. Some women overspend their credit cards because they've worked hard and they deserve it. For me it's a glass, or two, or three of wine at the end of the day, because, goddammit, I deserve it.

Well, I'm paying for it now; if it's going to kill me to get up and brave the cold for an hour to give the dog a good walk, then it serves me right.

✕ ✕ ✕

The weather has chosen to match my mood almost perfectly. There's a damp grey mist moving in over the lake, a kind of tactile gloom that steals through my layers of clothing to prod at my ribs. I shove my hands into my jacket pockets and keep my eyes downcast, staring at my feet as they make slow progress along the frozen dirt road. It must have snowed again last night, just a dusting. Walking is treacherous now, with the icy ruts covered over with a layer of flurries—easy to slip, if you're not careful. Quiet out here, this time of day. The dog and I make tracks along the side of the road; everywhere else is pristine, untouched.

In a decidedly melancholy frame of mind, I make my way over the railroad tracks and further along the lakeshore. I don't see the old lady until I'm directly in front of her house. She's a tiny old thing kitted out in an outlandish combination of winterwear—a purple, oversized parka, bright red jogging pants, a knitted cap with ear flaps, and a long woolen scarf that's been wound two or three times around her neck, leaving enough material free to flap in the breeze. Standing just inside the iron fence that guards the little house two doors up from Tina's, she's hanging on to the collar of our friend, the noisy *displaced* PERSONS

Rottweiler, and I notice that for the first time since I arrived here, the gate is open. Quickly, I look around for Jake and see that he has continued up the road about twenty yards and is standing there, looking back, waiting for me.

This has to be Masha, the old woman who knew Tina; she waves vigourously in my direction, urging me to come over to the gate. Gingerly, I obey, not taking my eyes off her dog.

"Is it all right?" I ask, meaning will the dog let me approach, and she nods: Yes, yes, come, it is all right. Then she says something to the dog in another language and although he keeps straining to get free, he does stop barking.

"Your dog," she says, once I'm standing next to her, letting her animal get used to the smell of me, "he can come, Ivan will not hurt him."

"Thanks, but I don't think so. He won't come over, but it's okay—he won't run off. He's an old dog and he stays pretty close."

Again, she says a few words to her dog and straightens up, letting go of his collar. I'm prepared for him to take off after Jake but instead he sits down, yawns and begins to scratch at an itch behind his right ear. As for the older woman, she stands approximately as high as my shoulder; she may even be shorter, without the cap.

"So this is Ivan," I say. "Hello, Ivan."

Holding out my hand to the woman, I introduce myself.

"My name is Alex. And you must be Masha."

She grins, showing a row of teeth too perfect to be real, and wrinkles her eyes at me, squinting to get a better look. Close up like this, she appears to be not quite as old as I first thought—in her early seventies, perhaps. Not ancient. Her skin is scrubbed and only faintly wrinkled and the wisps of hair which have struggled free of that ridiculous cap are a dark, chestnut brown.

"You know me," she says, pleased. "People tell you about me?" Without waiting for an answer, she continues: "I live here long time, very long time. Everybody knows Masha—she is famous."

I agree that she is, indeed, famous and that I've been wanting to talk to her, but she interrupts me: "Your dog is sick," she says, and my obvious surprise brings another gratified smile to her face. "I know these things, I see your dog down here these months. Lately I can see he is not well. I have something for him."

I notice that she says she's seen my dog down here, not, "I see *you* down here." Obviously she's watched me carry out my daily reconnoitering of the area, but she's chosen to introduce herself today because of the dog. Now she tells me I must come in. Jake's chosen instead to settle in a dry spot under a fir tree, just off the road—I may be willing to take my chances with this strange dog and his owner but he definitely is not.

"He'll be all right," I tell her. "He won't go far. But I shouldn't leave him for very long."

This isn't good enough for Masha. She shakes her head, takes hold once more of Ivan's collar, and leads him to a large kennel a few feet inside the fence, where he immediately flops down on the ground and begins gnawing on a bone. Slipping in through the back door of her house, she reappears momentarily with a leash and collar. This, I gather, is for Jake. Ignoring my protests that he won't come any closer, the older woman leaves the yard and strides purposefully down the road, calling out softly to the dog, who sits up and watches her approach with interest. In a moment she's bending down beside him, stroking his head and back and, although I can't hear from where I stand just outside the gate, she seems to be speaking to him. He nuzzles against her and allows her to slip the collar over his neck and fasten it.

The next thing I know, Masha is retracing her steps with Jake calmly following along beside her. She leads him into the yard and tells me to come in, and once I've done so, she closes the gate and locks it. Ivan has lost interest in us, so the three of us walk unmolested down the narrow path that bisects her tiny backyard. Once inside, she removes her scarf, cap, and jacket and hangs them on a wooden peg next to the door, indicating that I should do the same. Minus all that winter paraphernalia, she seems even tinier than before, a little doll of a woman with a frizz of short, curly hair that I can now see has been dyed a startling shade of reddish-brown.

"Come," she says, as I fumble with my winter boots. "Sit in kitchen. I make us some tea."

First, however, she attends to the dog. Leading him over to where a large tin bowl sits on the floor, filled with clean water, she urges him to drink. He takes a few laps, just to be polite, then looks around the room expectantly. This is a treat, a chance to investigate new surroundings, but before he can begin a detailed reconnaissance, Masha takes him gently by the collar and leads him over to a chair next to mine.

"Sit," she tells him, and for once he does just that. Her hands on each side of his head, she studies his face for a few minutes, looking into his eyes and speaking to him softly, in a foreign language. Hungarian, I think—Nadine said she was originally from Hungary. Finally, she nods, as if what she has seen has confirmed what she already knew, gives him a pat on the head and tells me he's been sick for two months, maybe three.

"Yes," I begin, "the vet said—"

"You sit down," she says. "We will have tea, then I give you something."

"I don't know, Masha. He's on medication. I don't think I should be giving him any more drugs."

"Drugs!" She hurls the word through her perfect teeth with a look of sheer disgust. "Drugs are for sick, not for staying well. I can help. But first, the tea."

As she moves around her tiny kitchen, which is immaculate and almost monastic in its sparseness, she begins to pepper me with questions: Where am I from? What am I doing out here? Why do I walk down this way almost every morning? What am I hoping to find? I tell her as much as she wants to know, holding back very little. If I'm forthright with this woman, it's possible she'll tell me what she knows about Tina.

It turns out that Masha remembers her very well, recalls that she was an unhappy young woman, with many bad friends hanging around. Most of all, Masha remembers Shadow, Tina's German shepherd. The dog, she tells me, was neglected—Tina left him alone for days on end, and the poor thing would have starved to death if Masha had not fed it, brushed the burrs out of its coat. When Tina died, no one wanted the dog; he might even have been put down, if her mother and sister had their way, which would have been a crime because he was a good dog, and young—no more than six or seven. So Masha took him in, and he lived to be fifteen, which is a very respectable age for a big dog like that.

When our tea is ready, we sit down at the small, oval table in the kitchen and drink from hand-thrown pottery mugs on which cobwebby leaves in shades of amber, gold, and ochre have been painted with a fine-grained brush. Masha's daughter is an artist and she has made all the dishes in the house. She has brought out a plate—the leaf theme, again, this time in vivid reds and yellows—on which she has placed a half-dozen sticky buns that she tells me are fresh from the oven this morning. The dog, too, gets a bun—just one, but he plants himself at her feet, encouraged to see if the treat will be repeated.

Settled with our tea and buns, I ask her what else she
remembers of Tina. Without hesitation she tells me that Tina
was very beautiful, and friendly. She came over to Masha's
house to get her dog whenever she'd been away for a while and
was always very grateful that Masha had taken him in.
Sometimes she would sit and talk about her job—when Masha
first knew her, Tina was working in the mental hospital, where
they put the crazy people. Crazy old people who had nobody to
look after them, sometimes they ended up in the mental place.
Which was why Masha had built her fence, and why she let her
dog bark at strangers. You never knew who might be planning
to come out to the lake and take you away. You couldn't trust
anybody.

Steering her back to the topic at hand, I ask her about
Conrad—did she know him at all? Had she ever seen him
around?

She shakes her head: No, she didn't see any of these people
who came out here in those days. She never went over to Tina's
camp except when she heard the dog barking for a long time;
then she knew the girl had gone away again and the dog was
hungry. And lonely. And when Tina came to get Shadow, she
always came alone. She talked about her young man, though,
sometimes. She said he was good-looking but he had problems—he drank too much and took too many drugs. They all
did, the people who came out here back then. Many, many times
the police were out here, asking questions of the neighbours.

"Did the police ever talk to you?" I ask.

"Oh, yes," she says, "lots of times. But I have nothing to say
to them. In Old Country you don't talk to police."

We sip our tea in silence, and she strokes the dog in an
absent-minded fashion. Abruptly, as if she's been waiting to
talk about this for a very long time, she says it was she who

found Tina's body. She heard the gunshot, went over to Tina's house two doors away and found the girl lying there on the floor, bleeding to death. She, Masha, called the police and waited for them to arrive, sitting out on the steps with poor Shadow because it was too terrible, what had happened inside. I don't interrupt.

＊ ＊ ＊

The girl had been in a bad way the week before she died, Masha says. She was missing the boyfriend, the one who had died, and she was afraid. The roadway leading to her camp was filled with cars and motorcycles almost every night. The nights when her friends were not there, she would arrive at Masha's doorstep and ask to come in and have tea—she couldn't sleep. This was before Masha had had the fence built at the back, and Tina would just appear at the back door with her dog. The two of them would sit in the front room and drink tea, and the girl would cry because of missing the boyfriend. Sometimes, when Masha went to bed, the girl would curl up on the sofa, and Masha would find her there in the morning, asleep with the dog at her feet.

The second week in September it started to rain, and it rained for two days, maybe three. Lots of the camps closer down to the lake were flooded. Masha was on higher ground, so she stayed dry, but the wind tore down branches and the waves scattered the beach with pieces of driftwood.

On the third day, Tina's dog began to bark around noon, and the barking continued, off and on, for an hour. Masha tied a scarf around her head, put on her oversized rain slicker and went out to investigate. Shadow was tied up outside, soaking wet and hungry, as usual; there was no sign of the girl. After pounding on the door and receiving no answer, Masha made her way through the mud and broken branches to the side of the house and rapped on the bedroom window. After what seemed a very long time, Tina's sleepy face appeared at the window, and Masha called out to her to come and open the door. The girl stared at her through eyes heavy with sleep; she seemed confused. Finally, Masha managed to get through to her. She came to the door and unlocked it, standing there like a ghost, her hair in disarray, her lips pale and slightly bruised.

Without waiting for an invitation, Masha entered the cabin, and found a towel to give Shadow a rubdown. Once the dog was relatively dry, she brought him into the kitchen, gave him food and water and looked around for a kettle to make some tea. Tina watched the older woman dig under the sink and come up with a small saucepan, minus the handle, which would serve to boil water. The kitchen was in chaos—there was no sign of food anywhere, but the residue of one long, never-ending wake was in evidence: cigarette butts, empty wine and beer bottles, puddles of booze on the floor, the coffee table, the kitchen counter. Masha assumed those so-called friends had been out here again last night, and the party had gone on well into the morning.

Once she had settled Tina on the couch with a mug of tea and a blanket, and laid down a blanket for the dog to settle at her feet, Masha prepared to leave. Tina didn't want to be alone; she begged Masha to stay. But Masha had things to do; she told the girl to come to her house at six o'clock. She'd make soup and bread; they'd have dinner together. Tina nodded: Yes, she would come.

Masha spent the rest of that afternoon picking up garbage scattered all over her property, stacking the driftwood to use later, when it dried out, for firewood. At regular intervals she tended to the soup simmering on top of her stove, beet soup cooked with red peppers and roasted garlic. Just the food to recover from the kind of soaking they'd had. By five o'clock the soup was ready. Masha turned off the stove and lay down for a nap, just for an hour or so until supper. She slept longer than she intended.

When she awoke, it was dark outside. Tina was banging frantically on her back door. The girl had undergone some sort of transformation since she had last seen her: she was raving, almost hysterical, and close to collapse. Masha tried to get her to sit down, tried to find out what was wrong, but Tina could not put words into complete sentences. She wanted to use the phone; her own was out of service. Masha pulled up a stool to where the ancient black telephone hung on the wall, dialed the number scribbled on a piece of paper Tina gave her—area code 604, which meant Vancouver.

While the girl waited for someone to pick up the phone at the other end, Masha turned on the stove and prepared to reheat the soup. She should call somebody, but who? It was Saturday night and who would come out here in the dark? Someone out in Vancouver had picked up the phone, and Tina was telling them that people were trying to kill her. They had come out to her camp and tried to run her over with her car, left her for dead under her car. She slipped and fell off the stool, and Masha helped her up; it was as if she was drunk but Masha did not think she'd been drinking—there was no smell of it, for one thing. She was simply limp, like a rag doll, and unable to stop crying.

When Tina got off the phone, Masha tried to get her to eat, have some soup, but no, the girl wanted to go home, she wanted to lie down in her own bed. This, Masha thought, was maybe the best thing after all: she needed sleep, and if she slept long enough she might wake up the next morning with the demons swept out of her head.

So Masha helped her back to her cabin—she was like a helpless old lady, stumbling in the dark, leaning against Masha who was half her size. The dog ran back and forth between them and the little house. And all the time Tina was crying, telling Masha over and over that they were going to kill her, the boyfriend was dead and soon she would be, too. Who was going to kill her, who were these people? But the girl wouldn't say. Or couldn't. Masha hushed her as you would try to calm a small child, led her into her house where all the lights were blazing, got her into bed and saw that Shadow was settled on the floor, next to her. Quietly, she went around turning off the lights, leaving one burning in the kitchen, just over the stove. She could hear the girl crying in her bedroom, still talking about dying and about the boy, as if she had a fever. When the older woman felt there was no more she could do, she retied her scarf around her head and went home.

The gunshot, when she heard it, sounded several hours later. Masha knew immediately where it came from. She found her flashlight and hurried out into the dark—she could hear the dog barking from inside the cabin. The door was shut but not locked. She stepped inside and the dog rushed towards her, threw his body against her and almost knocked her off her feet. She bent down to pat him and as she did so, she saw two bare feet on the bedroom floor. Slowly, not wanting to see what she knew she would see, Masha stepped forward. The girl was there, crumpled into a heap on the dirty green carpet. Blood was everywhere.

Without turning around, keeping her eyes on that terrible, shattered figure lying there, Masha backed out of the doorway and retraced her steps. When she got back to her own place, she

Margie Taylor

picked up the phone and dialed 911. And then, knowing it might be a while before they got there, Masha went back to the little house two doors down, and sat on the front step in the dark with the dog, waiting for the police.

᙮ ᙮ ᙮

This is as much as Masha remembers about that night, or as much as she is willing to tell me. As for what may or may not have happened after she left Tina, after she put her to bed and left her there, willing her to sleep, the older woman shrugs: Who knows, it was all a long time ago. She did hear a car head up the road—or a truck maybe, it was hard to be sure—shortly after the noise of the gun. It sounded as if it could be coming from Tina's house, but by the time she had found the flashlight and put on her rubber boots, there was no sign of anyone on the road. Yes, she had told the policemen, but they hadn't seemed interested. The two men who came, they were young, they were impatient to get through this and get back to town. A suicide, they said, even before the ambulance arrived.

The mother and the other one, the sister, they said it was something else, they came out to talk to Masha, but there was nothing she could tell them. The mother was a crazy lady: she wanted Shadow put down, she said the dog should be with her daughter, but Masha shut the door in her face and refused to give him up: the dog had done nothing, why should he be punished? So Shadow stayed with her. The following spring, she had men from town come out and build a strong, steel fence across the back of her property.

Jake has fallen asleep at our feet. I thank Masha for taking the time to talk to me. Then she tells me she has something for me—she leaves the room and returns with a jam jar containing a pale green liquid that smells, when she pries off the lid, of something pleasant and familiar, although I can't put a name to it. Masha says it's a tonic she's created, a blend of herbs grown here in her kitchen—one tablespoon three times a day and the dog will soon be feeling better. Again, I thank her and slip the jar into my coat pocket, resolving to call Dr. Jim on Monday and see what he thinks. But we're not finished: Masha wants to be paid for the tonic, as it turns out. Ten dollars, no sales tax. I have no money on me but she assures me that's all right, I can drop it off the next time I come by. I look like a good person; she'll trust me. No cheques, though, just cash. Masha never goes near banks, which are all run by Jews who steal your money. It seems like an excellent time to leave.

25

W HEN THE CAR—MY CAR—PULLS UP TO THE DOOR
shortly before two o'clock, it takes me by surprise; I have completely forgotten Gavin's telephone call earlier this morning.
Normally Jake would be barking furiously at the arrival of a tres-
passer, but the events of the day have exhausted him. He doesn't
budge from where he's curled up and fallen asleep in the chair
next to the window.

Gavin McCormick is standing a few steps from the car,
looking out over the lake, as if he's found something unusual
on the horizon. The mist has lifted and the sky has become that
clear, luminous shade of winter blue I remember from my
childhood, almost too bright to look at directly, but reflected in
the snow. The skies over the west coast in all their vaporous
beauty never shine like this. I've missed the vitality of this sunlight. I imagine this is the kind of sky that might hang over the
Australian outback, or the Sahara.

"Beautiful day." He has turned towards me and is moving
up the little walkway towards the front steps. Liz, he tells me,
decided she wasn't up to the drive. "When I left, she was flat on
her back in bed with a hot water bottle. She says to give you her
love. She'll call you later in the week."

Unlike Liz and myself, this man seems in the best of health.
His cheeks are ruddy and in the afternoon light he seems
younger than he did the night before. Perhaps because of the
way he's dressed: last night he wore a relatively sober business
suit and tie, today he's in a leather jacket, jeans, and sneakers. A
boy squeezed reluctantly into the carapace of a grown man,
retaining the awkward grace of youth. He *is* attractive, dammit.

Instinctively, I run my fingers through my hair, wishing I'd remembered he was coming.

He says he brought something for me, reaches into his pocket and extracts a set of car keys. *My* car keys. I thank him and he says, "No, not those, I brought you something else."

Reaching into his other pocket, he pulls out a video cassette: *The Sound of Music.*

"Oh. Thank you. But I'm not sure I'll get a chance to watch it before I leave. There's no VCR out here."

"You don't have to. I bought it for you. Watch it when you get back to Vancouver."

While we're talking, he's come up the steps and into the cabin. He stands for a moment, gazing around the room, appraising his surroundings. I refrain from saying anything about the prints and wall hangings until he's had a chance to take a look at a couple of them close up, at which point he judges them to be quite good and wants to know if I painted them.

Once again, as I did with Dr. Jim, I admit that no, they belong to the couple who owns the place. He nods and does a complete stroll around the room, stopping now and then to study one or two of them, the way you would in an art gallery or museum. In order to avoid standing by like the curator or security guard, I offer to make a cup of tea.

"You wouldn't have any coffee, would you?"

"No, sorry. I've run out."

He nods morosely and says tea would be fine. "Don't women drink coffee any more?" he wonders. "I mean, unless it's laced with liquor or sold at some fancy place where you have to be able to speak Italian to order it? I can't remember the last time I was offered a cup of coffee in a woman's apartment."

This last comment conjures up so many immediate, uncomfortable associations I decide it might be safer to change the subject. "It was good of you to drive all the way out here," I tell him, filling up the kettle and placing it on top of the stove. "You really didn't have to do it, though. I could have taken a cab into town."

"I haven't been out this way in years. I wanted to see what it looks like these days. It hasn't changed a whole lot, has it?"

"It seems very different to me. But then it's been twenty years since I spent any time out here. The houses are bigger, for one thing. And there's more of them."

Gavin has seated himself at one end of the sofa, leaving me with the option of sitting beside him, heaving the sleeping dog out of the seat by the window or taking the only other chair in the room, the uncomfortable objet d'art. I opt for the objet, and decide to get the hard stuff over as soon as possible.

"Gavin, I have to tell you, I'm really sorry for the way I behaved last night. It was unforgivable and I wouldn't want you to think—"

He stops me. "Don't be silly. We were celebrating. We all drank more than we should have."

"No, I don't mean that. I'm talking about—well, you know."

Suddenly I can't continue. I feel like a fool. Unless, of course, he doesn't remember. There's just a slim possibility that he might have been a little drunk himself and may have forgotten my attempt to seduce him under the restaurant table.

What he says next catches me completely off guard: "I know what you're talking about, Alex. I repeat, we were all in what you might call a festive mood. What I would like to know is, were you serious?"

"I beg your pardon?"

There is something comical about the scene. He sits there on the sofa, completely relaxed, absolutely in control of the situation, while I perch uncomfortably across from him, feeling like I'm back in school again, in the principal's office. Gavin has taken on an authoritative manner—the boy grown up and put in charge, his kindly manner containing a hint of steel.

"I'm sorry, Gavin, you've lost me. You want to know if I was serious? Serious about what?"

He leans forward and rubs his hands together, perhaps only to warm them—it's cool in here—but the gesture strikes me as betraying an underlying excitement. What the hell is he getting at?

"Alex." He pauses as if reflecting on the sound of my name, then says it again, softening it this time: "Alex, I have to tell you—I'm a romantic when it comes to women. Good-looking women especially, with great legs. Tell me something."

And now he glances down at my legs, as if visualizing them as they were last night, without the jeans and battered old sneakers.

"Do you ever wear stockings?"

Feeling myself flush, and hating myself for it, I respond that yes, sometimes I do.

He nods. "I thought so. You really do have terrific legs. I'd love to see them in nylons sometime."

I say nothing, there's no suitable response to this. And then he makes the pitch:

"You know, Alex, I live in the world of business but I act on impulse a good deal of the time. It's probably childish, but there are many things about childhood we shouldn't give up, and one of them is going after things we want. I travel a lot and I'm in Vancouver two or three times a year. I would very much like to be allowed to call you the next time I'm there and—get to know you better."

The kettle begins to boil; with relief, I push myself out of the chair and head into the kitchen.

"I'll take mine black," Gavin announces, as if he hadn't just been proposing some kind of intermittent, illicit affair. And perhaps he hadn't. Perhaps I've gotten it wrong.

When I return with two mugs of tea and set them down on the coffee table, he smiles up at me and picks up where he left off.

"So, Alex, what do you think? Will we get a chance to see each other the next time I'm in Vancouver?"

There is potential here for misunderstanding, for getting things wrong. When I was younger I almost never got it wrong. I used to know exactly when a man was attracted to me, when he was coming on to me. Now I'm like a cat with its whiskers cut off—I've lost my antennae for these sorts of things.

Carefully, keeping my voice light and casual, I say, "Are you saying you want to see me as in going out for a cup of coffee? Do you want to drop by the house when you're there, meet my husband? Stay for dinner?"

He smiles and lifts the mug to his lips. There's a self-satisfied delineation to the contours of that mouth I hadn't noticed before. This is a man who believes he already knows how the movie will end.

"Meet your husband," he says, as if considering the possibility. "Well, perhaps I wouldn't want to go that far. But I would definitely like to spend some time with you *without* the company of your husband." He puts the mug down and leans forward. "There's this terrific little place I know out in White Rock, right by the ocean, a little bed and breakfast run by a couple of British expats. It's far enough away that we wouldn't run into anyone. And the couple who own it are very discreet. So what do you say? Would you be up for it?"

All right, mystery solved. It's obvious now what he's talking about and knowing this, I know exactly what to say. Smiling, feeling relaxed now in spite of the chair, I explain that my actions last night were foolish and impulsive. I'd drunk far too much and was simply following up on a whim. I certainly wouldn't want him to go around thinking I act that way as a usual thing—

He interrupts me; the principal has listened to as much of the story as he needs, in order to confirm what he already knew.

"Alex." (I've never had anyone use my name as often in a regular conversation. I almost expect him to come out with the full epithet, as my English teacher used to do: "Alexis Elizabeth Cooper, what *exactly* are you trying to say?")

"It's all right, Alex. I know exactly what was happening last night."

"You do?"

"Of course. You've been married for a long time, and things have gone a little stale. From what you told me last night, I assume the spark's been gone for quite a while, right? Listen, I've been there myself. I know exactly what you're going through. I like what Disraeli had to say about marriage—do you know the quote? 'It destroys one's nerves to be amiable every day to the same human being.' Wonderful, isn't it?"

"Gavin—"

"And of course you've been out here on your own for, what, three months? That's a long time. It's natural that you'd be feeling a little lonely and be wanting companionship. It's perfectly understandable."

I have an overpowering urge to slap him across one of his pink, well-preserved cheeks, but I hold myself back and simply tell him, in a firm, Mother-knows-best voice, that he's taken it the wrong way. We will not be getting together, not in White Rock or anywhere else. Even if I was attracted to him—which I am not—Liz Murray is one of my very best friends and I would never go behind her back like that. There, that's the end of it. Relieved at having got this over and done with, I pick up the teapot.

"More tea, Gavin? There are some cookies if you're hungry."

He waves the teapot away with a brief, dismissive gesture. "Don't be a child, Alex. It doesn't become you. You're old enough to know what's going on. Let's not waste time playing games."

"I'm not playing games and I'm not a child," I say, feeling very childlike. "And don't patronize me."

To my alarm, he stands up and comes over to my side of the coffee table, takes me by the hand and pulls me to my feet. Out of the corner of my eye I can see that the dog, disturbed by this, has woken up and is gazing warily in our direction. Something unusual is going on. Unusual enough to make Jake sit up and take notice. Gavin has yet to see him.

"We don't have to wait till Vancouver, you know," Gavin says, keeping hold of my hand and staring intently into my eyes. "We have the perfect opportunity right now to see how we feel about each other."

"Are you suggesting—"

"I'm suggesting we go into your bedroom, wherever that is, shut the door and make love to each other. Can you think of a better way to spend a beautiful winter afternoon, out here by the lake?"

"We could go ice fishing."

The joke, such as it is, falls flat. Gavin doesn't see this as a laughing matter, although for some reason it's beginning to seem increasingly amusing to me. Here I am, standing practically nose to nose with a man I barely know (whose breath, by the way, smells of toothpaste or a mint-flavoured mouthwash) with my hands clasped together in his as if he were about to arrest me. I still have it in my head somehow that I can joke him out of this.

"Gavin, this is absurd. I am not going to have sex with you. And anyway, what about Liz? She's my friend—can you imagine how she'd feel if she knew you were out here suggesting we climb into bed together?"

Again, the knowing, avuncular smile. "*If* she knew," he repeats. "But she isn't going to, is she? I hardly think either of us is going to run to Mommy and tell her that we've been naughty. I think we're a little more grown-up than that."

I attempt to move to one side, hoping he'll release me; keeping me firmly in his grip, Gavin follows my movements, studying my face with an intensity meant to intimidate me.

"Gavin—please, let me go. This is silly—"

I take a backward step, and then another, and immediately we are caught up in a kind of sexual *danse macabre* with myself in the lead, him following, around the coffee table until, unable to see where I'm going, I trip over the rug and fall back on to the sofa. Gavin lands squarely on top of me.

At first I'm willing to give him the benefit of the doubt—it was an accident, I fell and he, holding on to my hands, was brought down too. He releases my hands, and I begin to apologize for my clumsiness, but almost immediately he goes to work, pulling at the zipper on my jeans and reaching under my sweater to grab at my breasts.

"Gavin, for God's sake, get off me!"

He doesn't appear to have heard me. His head is buried in my chest, revealing a perfect circle of skin the size of a quarter at the top of his head. He's saying my name—moaning it, rather, and struggling to pull down my pants. His head moves further down, his dry lips press against my stomach and the fabric of my underpants. I watch with a kind of bemused detachment as he noses around my crotch like a dog in heat.

There's no getting around it: to all intents and purposes, I'm being seduced, perhaps even raped. But I can't summon the proper feelings of fear, panic, or anger. The situation is simply too ridiculous; the couch, for one thing, is too small to accommodate us properly. My back is twisted at an uncomfortable angle, which reminds me of back-seat necking in my teens. There has been not even a hint of foreplay or wooing on his part (also reminiscent of those back-seat necking sessions), and I can't help wondering if he'll give himself a stroke carrying on like this. Joan told me he had a lot of stamina, sexually speaking, but he's going at things in such a mad rush I'm tempted to tell him to slow down and take a breather.

Suddenly, he rears up and begins to fumble with his belt buckle. My senses kick in: this man means business. He actually intends to fuck me, right here on the couch. I try to push him off me, but for a slim man he's heavier—and stronger—than I would have thought. I reach up towards his face, intending, I guess, to grab him, rake his skin with my fingers, but he catches my hand in his and holds on to it with one hand it while continuing to undo his belt and pull down his zipper with the other. I turn my head to see what there might be close at hand—an ashtray—something—on the coffee table or the floor that I could use to smash against his head, when suddenly the dog leaps from the window seat and lands directly in front of us, growling and baring his teeth.

Gavin is brought to an immediate halt as he stares at the dog. One hand still on his belt, he asks, "What the hell is that?" I can see he is attempting to gauge the potentiality of danger. An angry, snarling dog, whose teeth seem in remarkably healthy condition. He is also ill and overweight, but Gavin doesn't know that.

"Good boy," he says, and brings a hand down towards the dog's head.

"I wouldn't do that," I say, and Gavin snatches his hand back.

"He can be very nasty when he's in this mood. I mean it, Gavin, he can really be vicious. He once ripped a hole in the leg of a door-to-door salesman who was getting pushy with me." God forgive me for so blatantly lying about the world's most mild-mannered animal.

My would-be lover is unsure what to do. Obviously, having got this far, he's reluctant to give up and go home, but there is the matter of the dog.

"Put him in the bedroom," he says. I look at him and laugh. The moment of panic is gone; we're back to situation comedy again.

"You must be joking. That dog won't budge until you're out of here. And if you think I'm going to try to get him to do anything when he's in this kind of mood, well, you can think again."

As if to back me up, the dog gives a particularly threatening snarl and begins to bark, keeping his liquid brown eyes fixed on Gavin. On Gavin's belt, to be exact. Because it is, after all, the belt that has brought all this on. For years David has been careful to undress where the dog can't see him—a fact that Gavin doesn't know and I'm not about to tell him. Carefully, keeping his eyes on the dog, he lifts one leg over the far side of the sofa and clambers down to the floor where he stands for a moment, unsure of his next move.

I take advantage of this to sit up and adjust my clothing. Before Gavin can say anything, I suggest he might want to get the hell out of there before the dog makes a lunge for his throat. Because the dog is still barking, and doesn't look at all close to relaxing his guard and going back to sleep. After a moment's

Margie Taylor

hesitation, Gavin picks up his jacket from the floor and slowly, walking backward, makes his way to the door.

"I'll call you," he says, just as I slam the door in his face and lock it.

The offending belt buckle is out of sight; the dog sits back on his haunches, scratches one ear and yawns, as if frightening off potential rapists is all in a day's work.

"Good boy."

I reach down to stroke his lovely old head and slump down on the floor beside him. And then, sitting there, my arms around an old dog who is taking the opportunity to lick my cheek, I start to laugh. I laugh till tears come to my eyes, picturing Gavin on top of me, furiously gnawing away at my crotch, grabbing at my breasts as if he were squeezing melons in the supermarket.

"Oh, God, Jake," I ask, when I can finally catch my breath, "was sex always this funny?"

※ ※ ※

Much later, towards the end of the afternoon, I am straightening up the living room, having taken a bath and put in a call to the kids. Both of them. Just to make sure they're all right. I gather up the discarded tea mugs from the coffee table and take them over to the kitchen counter and notice my car keys. Only then does it dawn on me to wonder how Gavin got himself back to town. In my mind's eye, I see him standing by the highway, hitchhiking. I hope that's what happened. There's something just a little ridiculous about hitching a ride once you're over thirty.

26

JOAN IS LEAVING TOMORROW TO SPEND A MONTH with her mother in Florida. She's dreading it, says she cannot imagine how she'll get through four weeks in the same place with that woman.

"She'll start on me the minute I get in," she says. "My weight, of course. 'Why do you let yourself get so heavy? Can't you go on a diet or something? You won't get a man looking like that.' Oh, God, it's going to be awful. And Max will hate it—he hates flying, for one thing. He'll sulk right through Christmas because of that."

"Maybe you shouldn't go."

"I have to. The alternative is hanging around the house thinking up new ways *not* to think about Gavin. And I'm running out of ideas. I've just got to get out of here."

After that, she says, she's coming back, putting the house up for sale and moving to Toronto.

"You'll miss that house."

"I know," she says. "I think I always had it in the back of my mind that one day Gavin and I would live there together. And now that I see that's not going to happen—"

She shrugs.

"I think you're being very brave."

Joan's mouth twists in a wry attempt at a smile. "It doesn't have much to do with bravery. It's more about not having a choice."

"You have a choice. You could stay on here and wait for him to get tired of Liz and maybe decide to come back. And you're not. You're getting on with your life, and I think that's brave.

You should feel good about it, Joan. You *do* feel good about it, don't you?"

Instead of answering directly, she tells me she thinks she's reached a point in her life where she's willing to rely more on herself than on a man. Or on anybody.

"I mean, I trust me," she says. "I've been living with me for fifty years—who else do I know this well? I'm not always crazy about me, but at least I know what I'm getting. No surprises— didn't that used to be the slogan for the Holiday Inn? When I was younger I thought 'no surprises' meant boring and unadventurous. Now I just think it stands for a good place to sleep."

"What will you do in Toronto?"

"Well, I'll have my dad, of course. I've been looking into nursing homes there and when I find a good one, I'll move him, too. That way I can still see him a few times a week. Not that he'll notice, but it's important to me. What about you? What have you decided to do?"

I take a deep breath and come out with it. "I'm going back to Vancouver. On the weekend."

"Good," she says. "I'm happy for you."

"You don't seem surprised."

"I'm not. I had a feeling that's what you'd do."

"It doesn't mean anything, you know. It doesn't mean we're going to be able to work things out. It just means we're going to try."

The waitress comes over to our table with a couple of dessert menus in her hand.

"Well, ladies, what'll it be?" she asks. "Are you going to have dessert today or just coffee, as usual?"

I tell her I guess she knows us pretty well by now and she says, "Well, I should. You've been coming in here every Tuesday for, like, two months."

"Gosh, aren't we boring and predictable?"

"I don't think so. I think it's nice, having lunch with your girlfriend every week. More people should do that." The waitress leans forward and adds, in a confidential tone, "You know, I hope you don't mind me saying this, but I hope when I'm your age, I have a best friend I can talk to like you do, and get together every week like this."

Ignoring the reference to our advanced age, I tell her this is our last lunch, that Joan is heading down to Florida tomorrow and I'm going back to Vancouver.

"Really?" she says. "That's too bad. I'm sorry to hear that." She pauses, then adds, shyly, "I'm leaving too. I'm going back to school."

We congratulate her, and she confides that her parents have offered to help her out, if she moves back home. She seems flushed and happy, and we're happy for her; we've come to feel proprietary towards our waitress—whose name we still don't know.

Neither of us has mentioned Liz so far today, but now, in a tone that's a little too casual, Joan asks if I've heard from her.

"Actually, she called me last night."

She picks up a packet of Sweet 'n Low and rips it open in a careful, methodical manner, dumping the contents into a saucer.

"How is she?"

Get it out, Alex. Just say it and get it over with.

"They're going to Vegas for Christmas. He's getting a quickie divorce and they're getting married."

It had to be said but I wish like hell it wasn't me who had to say it. Joan reacts like she's been dealt a blow. She ducks her head, but not before I have a chance to see the look on her face.

"I'm sorry, Joan." And then, because I can't think of anything else to say, I say it again: "I really am just so sorry."

She shakes her head, grabs a napkin from the dispenser and waves a jewelled hand in the air, as if dismissing the subject.

"It won't last, Joan. I know I don't know him as well as you but something tells me he's not the kind of man who sticks around forever. He'll get bored and start having affairs. He hurt you, he probably hurt his wife, and I believe at some point he's going to hurt Liz."

"Maybe. You may be right. But don't tell Liz that. Let her enjoy it for now. She wouldn't believe you anyway and it'd just wreck your friendship. There are some things best kept to yourself, know what I mean?"

I know exactly what she means.

She reaches across the table and takes my hand. "I'm going to miss you," she says.

"I'll miss you too. Are you going to be okay?"

"Oh, sure," she says, smiling, stuffing the napkin in her pocket. "I'll be fine. It's just that what with Liz and Gavin and everything, and now you leaving, I guess I'm just feeling a little abandoned. You know?"

"I do know. I've been thinking that way myself. About me, I mean. But you're not being abandoned, neither of us are. We'll keep in touch, we'll write and talk on the phone. And Liz—well, she still cares about you, you know. She told me she was going to call you in January, and have you over for dinner before you leave."

Joan rolls her eyes. "Oh, God, I don't think so. I mean, I love Liz and all but it would just be too weird. Going over there for dinner with her and Gavin, and then me leaving alone and him staying. I don't think I'm modern enough to handle that, if you want to know the truth."

I agree with her. All this being great friends with your ex and his new wife or girlfriend, getting together for warm, touchy-feely dinners and so on—it's never appealed to me. At least in the old days, when you got dumped, you knew where you stood. You were not expected to put on a brave face at parties, or continue as if you were still the best of friends.

The waitress reappears bearing an enormous piece of chocolate cake upon which the word "Friendship" has been written in bright yellow icing. She sets it down in the middle of the table, and hands us each a fork.

Joan is as surprised as I am. We each assume the other has ordered this, but it turns out to be a parting gift from the waitress—our waitress. She looks a little embarrassed, but pleased with herself.

"Now, I know you ladies don't usually eat dessert, but I want you to go ahead and eat this, okay? Just this once. It's on me."

And then, as if she's worried she might have come across a little too assertively, she gives a quick smile and beats a retreat back to the kitchen.

I pick up my fork and nod towards Joan's. "Looks like we have no choice."

She smiles. "Looks like."

The cake is delicious, but if it tasted like sawdust we would have eaten it. It is, after all, an acknowledgment from youth that there is something to be celebrated about age and maturity. And more important—it's chocolate.

27

IT'S THE LAST DAY OF NOVEMBER AND I'M BACK TO wearing the light fall jacket I brought with me from the coast; temperatures have suddenly soared above normal. The ditches by the side of the road contain more water than snow. The road itself is a slurry of mud and gravel. In the old days this unexpected reprieve from winter would be hailed as good news for the shipping business: the boats could arrive into the harbour later, the economy would thrive. Now, with only a fraction of Canada's grain being shipped through Thunder Bay, the significance of the port has diminished; the elevators once important enough to appear on a national magazine cover now stand empty along the waterfront—unwanted eyesores, waiting to be demolished.

I reach the main road and wait for a pickup truck to pass. The driver slows down, so as not to splatter me with mud, leans out the window and calls out:

"Great weather, eh? Let's hear it for global warming."

I smile, wave, carry on, and eventually come to the small house with the large steel fence. Today, however, there is no sign of Ivan, the Rottweiler, and no response from Masha. I bang on the gate and call her name a couple of times, but she's either not home or not in the mood for company. Giving up, I slip an envelope with the ten dollars I owe her into her bright yellow mailbox and continue on my way.

The dog bounds ahead of me; when we reach Number 6, he heads directly down to the lake to investigate the beachfront. He's got energy today, a certain youthfulness. It seems to me he's been better for the past couple of days. Masha's tonic, perhaps? Then again, Dr. Jim said he'd have good days and bad days; this may simply be a good one. I cross my fingers and will him to hold on long enough to get back to Vancouver, for Kate's sake, who's been calling me every night, ostensibly to chat but in reality, I know, to check on the dog.

I have yet to come across any evidence of the current owner of this place. Whoever he is, he probably won't even think of the place until the spring; sometime in March or April he'll drive out from the city to check on winter damage: are there leaks in the roof, has anyone broken in over the winter? Until that point, I have as much right as anyone to claim it, and I suppose, over the past few months, I have.

Standing on the beach, gazing out at the water, I remember something Joan said—a remark she made when I told her David and I were going to try to sort things out. I said I wasn't sure it would work, that it all seemed pretty complicated. And she said, "We're humans, you know. Everything takes work. Life doesn't come tied up neatly into little brown packages; sometimes it's a little messy."

David and I were married the summer I graduated from university; we left Thunder Bay that fall. From time to time, through various friends, I heard things about Tina—that she and Ray had broken up, that she'd got her teaching certificate, that she'd been in trouble with the school board for passing bad cheques. And then, for a long time, I just didn't hear about her at all.

In the spring of 1976 my father was ill, and I flew back to Thunder Bay. I rented a car at the airport, drove directly to the hospital, and spent an hour in intensive care holding my father's hand while he slept. As I was leaving, I passed a gurney parked in the hallway. A young woman with short, curly blonde hair and an excess of makeup was lying on the trolley, eyes closed, a sheet pulled up to her chin. It was the blonde curls that did it. I stepped closer and took a better look.

"Tina? Is that you?"

The familiar blue eyes opened wide in alarm, and she raised a finger to her lips.

"Don't call me that," she whispered, darting a glance in the direction of the operating room. "For God's sake, keep your voice down. And don't call me Tina."

"Tina, is this some kind of joke—"

She cut me off. "Erika," she said, and when I appeared confused she added, "I'm using my first name—Erika. Not Tina."

"What are you doing here?"

I was sure it was some kind of joke—I mean, there she was, wearing a wig and far too much makeup, even for her—but she didn't crack a smile. Keeping her voice low and continuing to look around to see who might be listening, she said she was in for an abortion—a D and C, she said—and she'd been in just six months before and if they knew it was her they probably wouldn't let her have it. Which was why she was wearing the wig.

"Jesus, Tina—" She stopped me with a warning look. I lowered my voice and carried on. "You're going to hurt yourself if you carry on like this, you know that? Why the hell don't you use contraceptives?"

She rolled her eyes as if I should know better than to ask.

"The pill makes me fat," she whispered, "and the diaphragm is useless. I had an IUD, it hurt like hell, it just about killed me. So I had them take it out. And let me inform you, the rhythm method doesn't work."

A large nurse came striding by, crisply clad in white, carrying a clipboard. She cast a suspicious, disapproving stare in our direction and carried on.

"What have you told them?" I wanted to know. "The doctors and the staff here, what have you said?"

"I told them my name is Erika Davenport. It's my mother's married name—she got married again last summer. I told them I was raped and if I had to go through with the pregnancy, I'd kill myself."

"That's a bit extreme, don't you think?"

"It's what you have to do, don't you know? You have to convince them you're desperate. If they don't think you're about to jump off a building, they won't give the go-ahead."

I looked down at her, spread out under the starched green sheet, and thought how fragile she seemed in her hospital-issue gown and that ridiculous wig. I reached out and took hold of her hand, which startled her, I think. She looked up at me and frowned slightly. A tiny lock of her own dark hair was peeking through the blonde curls on her forehead.

"Tina—"

The frown deepened and I immediately corrected myself.

"Erika—sorry—are you going to be okay? Is there anything I can do?"

"What do you mean?"

"I don't know. I just thought there might be something— do you have a lift home? I mean, after?"

She smiled and made a quick adjustment to her curls, tucking the errant lock back under the wig.

"Oh, that's really sweet of you, Alex. But I'll be fine. Someone's coming to get me in a couple of hours. He's a TV producer—he says he can get me some work."

"That's terrific."

She nodded and made to look at her watch, forgetting she wasn't wearing one.

"What time is it?" she asked and when I said it was almost

three, she told me I'd better go. They'd be coming to wheel her into the OR any minute, she said.

On an impulse, I leaned down and gave her a kiss.

"It'll be all right," I said. "Everything will turn out okay."

She smiled. "I know that. Things always work out for me."

With that I released her hand, to the relief of both of us, I think, and wished her luck.

"Call me," she said. "We'll have a sauna together, out at the lake."

I nodded. "Sure, I'll do that."

I turned and walked toward the elevators. I never saw her again.

❊ ❊ ❊

The walk back seems longer than usual, partly because the dog is tired now and pauses frequently along the road. When we finally reach the cabin, I open the door and wait for him just inside the doorway. He hesitates at the bottom of the steps, contemplating whether or not he's up to the climb, and I wonder if I'm going to have to carry him into the house. He must weigh seventy pounds; I'm not sure I'd be able to manage it.

"Come on, boy, you can do it. Come on."

He hears the encouragement in my voice—as worn out as he is, his instinct is to please. I say it again and he makes his mind up to give it a try. Fatigue evident in every muscle, he lifts one old leg after the other and gets himself up the stairs, into the safety and comfort of our temporary home.

Does he even remember another? Are dogs like simple-minded children who adapt to new situations so completely their former circumstances are not merely forgotten but erased? I don't believe it. If he lasts long enough to make the

westward trip, he'll head directly to Kate's bedroom, plunk himself down on the familiar comforter and know that, after a long,
mysterious absence, he is home.

� ✗ ✗

*Just before twelve o'clock, the photographer declared that the light
was perfect.*

"A little to your left."

*She turned her head slightly, the grain elevators at the very edge
of her peripheral vision. The wind tossed her bangs, whipping a
strand of hair into her eyes; the winking assistant reached forward,
smoothed it back into place. Click. Click. Click. The motor of the
Nikon F whirred in the winter silence, six, seven times. She was cold,
her smile the grimace of an ice maiden, but she was prepared to sit
there pretending to play the cello forever. She was where she was
meant to be—finally—and she never wanted this moment to end.*

Author's Note

This book is a work of "faction"—fiction and fact—and I am
deeply indebted to several people for the facts. While working
on this book, I met with old friends, colleagues and some complete strangers for coffee or drinks, to discuss the events of the
summer and fall of 1977. I'd like to thank some of them here:

On two separate occasions, Bill Romanowski took the time
to share his memories about growing up in what he calls the
boon docks of Port Arthur, and led me on a walking tour to give
me a sense of the place.

The family of the late Walter Bober welcomed me into their
home and shared their photographs and recollections of their
brother and son.

I'm grateful to both Mickey Cashaback and Anna Gadd
who were generous with their time and their stories, as were
Fred Broennle and the late Harold Nordlander.

Dr. Lloyd Denmark, the deputy chief medical examiner for
the province of Alberta, provided me with valuable information
on investigating suicides and suspicious deaths. And lawyer
Don Colborne spent a morning explaining the intricacies of
Ontario's Freedom of Information legislation.

Rick Perkins helped me dig out some of the background
material and Fiona Karlstedt made introductions for me and
was unfailingly supportive, as always.

In Lynne Van Luven, I found the perfect editor—unstint-
ing in her efforts to pare back the layers to find the story, and
hugely generous with her time and encouragement. Thank
you, Lynne!

And thank you, too, to Bob Davies, who thought I should

go ahead and write the story in the first place; Ken Watts, who supported me while I dropped other work to do so; the board at NeWest Press, who saw the potential in the story, and Sarah and Jesse, who make everything worth while.